W9-AZO-286

Finding Danny

LINZI GLASS

Finding Danny

WALDEN POND PRESS
An Imprint of HarperCollins*Publishers*

Walden Pond Press is an imprint of HarperCollins Publishers.

Finding Danny
 For information address HarperCollins Children's Books, a division of HarperCollins Publishers, 10 East 53rd Street, New York, NY 10022.
www.harpercollinschildrens.com

Library of Congress Cataloging-in-Publication Data
Glass, Linzi Alex.
Finding Danny / Linzi Glass. — 1st ed.
p. cm.
Summary: While searching for her lost dog, Danny, twelve-year-old Bree meets Rayleen—a volunteer at the local animal shelter—who helps Bree put her life in perspective.
ISBN 978-0-06-179716-3
[1. Lost and found possessions—Fiction. 2. Dogs—Fiction. 3. Animal shelters—Fiction. 4. Santa Monica (Calif.)—Fiction.] I. Title.
PZ7.G481237Fi 2010 2009032054
[Fic]—dc22 CIP
AP

Typography by Andrea Vandergrift
10 11 12 13 14 CG/RRDB 10 9 8 7 6 5 4 3 2 1
❖
First Edition

For my friend Sylvia Kelegian, one of the many unsung animal rescuers, and for all the amazing dogs I have helped, and those I have yet to save

Chapter One

My life would have been completely different if my mom and dad had just decided to have another kid. Maybe a baby brother with freckles on his nose or a cute little sister whose giggles sounded like tinkling bells. But my parents must have felt that one gurgly bundle of joy fulfilled their "kid quota," and I was destined to be Sabrina "Bree" Davies, only daughter of Todd and Colleen, the superduo from Santa Monica, California.

Sure, being the "only one" had its perks—no sharing of toys, clothes, desserts, or bedrooms, no sibling squabbles, no "who's gonna use the bathroom first" races, and no yelling "it" to decide who got to sit in the front seat when Mom or Dad picked me up from school or the mall or a friend's house.

But while I didn't have to share my parents or anything in our home with another kid, I did have to share my parents with something that was very important to them both: their careers. Or "The News Monster," as I affectionately liked to refer to their jobs.

"They're journalists," is what I said when someone asked what my parents did for a living. "My mom's on TV and my dad's in print." The person asking would usually stare at me confused, but not wanting to sound stupid would say something like, "Wow, Bree, that must be so cool."

"Yeah, for them," I'd reply. "Colleen Davies, human interest television reporter; Todd Davies, hard news journalist for a big newspaper," I'd add if they wanted more juicy details.

"Awesome!" they'd say. But it wasn't awesome. News reporting took them both away, and always in an urgent, hurried way. In twelve years I can honestly say that the single most used word in our house was "deadline." And Mom and Dad were always racing toward it.

When I was three, I thought "deadline" was an evil witch with searing green eyes who might come and cast a spell on them both and I'd never see them again. So I would go to my room and play by myself with my Barbie dolls with missing patches of hair so the "deadline witch" wouldn't be mad at them. When I was seven, I imagined "deadline" as a neon pink rope that they had to race toward like in track, and if they made it across there would be a big prize—a two-week vacation for the whole family at a resort in Hawaii where the three of us could lie on the warm beach under palm trees that danced the hula all day in the balmy breeze. The best part would be that "deadline" wouldn't be allowed in Hawaii. It was banned on the islands.

But as I got older I realized that "deadline" was more like a never-ending escalator; one deadline just carried them to the next and the next and the next. And neither one of them ever got off.

I remember the second, the hour, the minute, and the day that "deadline" stopped mattering as much. It was the Saturday afternoon just a few days after my third-grade parent/teacher conference, which was what started everything.

"She's alone too much at home. The teachers say she's very social but seems a little lost. Eight is a hard age at best," I had heard them whispering to each other while I pretended to be asleep. "She should have something to call her own."

So the newsparents decided to add a fourth member to our team.

"Don't open up yet!" My mom had me sit on a sofa in the living room. I remember feeling the air-conditioning cooling the back of my neck while they got the "surprise" ready for me. As I squeezed my eyes shut, I could hear my dad's footsteps just a few feet away and a tiny little sound, like someone had stepped on a squeaky toy. Then my mom clapped her hands and shouted, "Okay, open up now!"

Right on the living room floor, in my dad's arms, was a puppy. Not just any puppy. The cutest puppy in the whole world. The most adorable thing I had ever seen. A black and white, fluffy, big-eyed, soft-whiskered border collie, the most perfect creature ever created.

I couldn't move. I just stared. It felt like a dream, but then the puppy made a little yip-yap sound and wriggled and I knew I was most definitely, one hundred percent wide awake. As he looked at me with his big round eyes, his little pink tongue came out of his tiny mouth. My dad stood and held him out to me and said, "He's all yours, kiddo," as he put the puppy in my arms. My mom sat down next to me on the sofa and placed an arm around my shoulders. "We decided you need a little friend at home. So, what do you think?"

Think? I couldn't think. I was feeling fur and softness and puppy breath on my cheeks as he licked me. I felt warm and woozy, the luckiest girl in the whole world. I held him tight.

"This is the best present you've ever given me, and it isn't even my birthday!"

My mom and dad hugged me at the same time, but not too hard because no one wanted the newest and smallest member of our family to get squashed.

I named him Danny, because if I'd had a baby sister or brother that would have been what I would have wanted her or him to be called. My best friends, Lulu and Kate, said it really wasn't a dog's name, but I didn't care. It suited him perfectly. Besides, being unique and different and special was what Danny-O turned out to be in every way.

He swam laps with me in our pool at six months, howled if you said the word "moon" and rolled over and played dead whenever I made the rat-tat-tat sound of a gun by the time he was three, and by his fourth birthday learned how to hold himself up on his back legs whenever I danced in the house.

Danny never left my side, from the minute I got home from school until I went to bed. He wagged his tail and jumped up to kiss me no matter whether he was tired or hungry or missed his walk because the deadline super-duo had forgotten his leash in a car that was parked at an airport or up on an embankment on the outskirts of Los Angeles where a brush fire was burning out of control. "*This is Colleen Davies from Channel Five reporting to you from Porter Ranch, where three thousand acres have already burned. . . .*"

Danny was my permanent sleepover snuggler, ball catcher extraordinaire, hairy headrest, lickfest for days, toe tickler, and yap monster, all rolled into one. And my dinner companion on nights when no one else was home.

"Spaghetti and meatballs. Your favorite." I rolled my fork around my plate as Danny sat looking up at me with those same big eyes that had stared at me for the first time all those years ago. He cocked his head and made the Danny half-woof, half-whine sound that meant he was getting impatient. I had already fed him two cups of kibble in his shiny silver bowl that was kept next to the water cooler, but I could never resist that look on his face. His tail wagged even before I put a giant meatball on a napkin and dropped it on the kitchen floor.

"Looks like it's just you and me, Danny-O, for this

very fine, heat-me-up-and-serve feast that the newsmom left in the fridge for us."

We had a housekeeper who came to clean, but she was usually gone by the time I got home from school. Sometimes my mom would pick me up, but when she couldn't I took the school bus home. That's when there'd be a note left and a dinner that needed to be zapped in the microwave because a news story had to be covered or she was running late at the station. My mom always signed the notes that she left taped to the front door for me with lots of XOXOs, but they didn't quite make up for not having her there, sitting across the table from me in person.

Danny gobbled down the meatball, then jumped up to lick the sauce off my face. "You're the best of the best. Do you know that, Danny-O?" I looked into his eyes as he put both paws on my shoulders. He held my gaze and gave a little bark as if to say, "Right. Exactly. Couldn't have said it better myself."

My dad had left to go overseas and would be gone for a few weeks, which was often how long his trips took. Wars and terrorist attacks were the things he covered most, which was weird since he was a really calm, no-drama kind of guy. Maybe that's why the newspaper sent him, because he had a cool head and could handle tense situations.

My mom came back about an hour later to find me and Danny snuggled on the living room couch reading *A Midsummer Night's Dream*. Danny had his head on my shoulder and I was trying really hard not to fall asleep. I had to learn the lines for Queen Titania in one of the scenes.

"I am so sorry I'm late, honey." My mom leaned down and gave me a kiss on the cheek and patted the top of Danny's head at the same time. She was still wearing her "news suit" and heels, but she pulled off her jacket and kicked off her shoes as she sat down beside me. "What have you two been up to?"

"Dinner, doing vocab words for English, and studying a scene from this play." I yawned. "Danny's been doing the lines of King Oberon. He's already got them down."

My mom laughed. "Told you we got you the smartest dog on the planet." I was about to tell her that actually the part of King Oberon was being played by a boy in my class, Ashton Adams, but her cell phone rang at that exact moment and she snapped it open and headed off to the kitchen.

I sighed. I never felt like I got more than little bits of time with my mom. Danny always seemed to know how I was feeling. He lay down and put his head in my lap. I bent over and kissed the fuzzy spot between his eyes.

One of the vocab words that I had to learn this week was "solidarity," and Danny and I were just that. A unit. Bound together. Forever.

"What would I do without you, Danny-O?" I whispered into his soft fur.

Chapter Two

Langston Middle School was located at the top of Mulholland Drive, with a guard gate and green lawns and playing fields ushering you in at the entrance. To get into the school I had gone through two interviews with the headmaster, and so had my parents. Mostly we were the kids of moms and dads in "the industry," as the television and film business is called. I'm pretty sure my dad was the only hard news journalist, but there were lots of kids whose parents were writers, producers, directors, and movie stars in Hollywood.

I didn't think there was anything special about us, but that was because I rarely met anyone from outside of my school. Just take my two best friends, Lulu Miller and Kate Sinclaire. Lulu's father was an agent and represented famous actors and actresses, and Kate's father was this well-known British producer who had worked with just about everyone. Lulu was a bit of a tomboy—no surprise with three older brothers—and had a stay-at-home mom, which was really lucky for her. Kate was an only child like me, and even though her mom didn't work either, she wasn't around all that much. Her mom's job, it seemed, was keeping herself looking young and beautiful by going to spas and salons in Beverly Hills all day. She once took me and Kate with her to get manicures and pedicures, and she was surprised when I told her my mom had never taken me before. Kate was starting to act more like her mom, and lately all she talked about was her latest seaweed body wrap and oxygen facial and deep tissue massage. Lulu and I had started wondering what had happened to the Kate we used to know.

"What about doing a fancy high tea at a hotel and we all have to dress up?" Lulu suggested as the three of us walked together to our next classes. It was so not Lulu to suggest a party like that. She must have been getting desperate and running out of ideas.

Kate shook her head and Lulu groaned, since this was the millionth suggestion that had been turned down. Kate's birthday was just a few weeks away and we had been debating what kind of party she should have for what felt like months.

"Karaoke in your family room and then a marathon movie night sleepover?" I said.

"Nah." Kate tossed her long blond hair back. "Something glamorous. Like a spa day in Beverly Hills. Manicures, pedicures, and everything. My mom thinks that's the best idea."

Lulu's dark, curly hair bounced vigorously. "Okay, whatever you say. It's your big day."

"Sure. That sounds fine," I said, wanting to get the whole birthday thing over with as the main topic of our conversations.

Lulu headed off to computer lab. As Kate and I walked in the direction of drama lab, I practiced my Queen Titania lines over in my head and realized I had a long way to go before I had them down.

I had been really shocked when Mr. Matheson, our supercool young teacher, paired me with Ashton Adams to work on a scene. Ashton was the very cute, ever popular son of a famous movie director who usually ignored me at school and had sighed loudly when Mr. Matheson made the announcement that we would be working together.

* * *

"Everyone will need at least two home rehearsals before presenting, so exchange numbers if you don't already have them and make a date to get together," Mr. Matheson said. We had to do a dry run-through of our lines sitting across from our partners on the small stage.

"Give us an Academy Award performance!" Max Benson, Ashton's best friend, shouted as we made our way to the front.

"Don't worry, I will!" Ashton looked back as I followed him and he gave one of his perfect white smiles to the rest of the class. I could almost hear all the girls in the room sigh together.

Ashton read his lines like a real professional, while I stammered and faltered a few times, then forced myself to stay focused. A "date" with Ashton seemed like a really unnerving idea since we had barely ever said more than five words to each other, despite the fact that we had most of our classes together. Now we would have to meet outside of school and spend time together. The thought made my stomach tighten into a knot that didn't loosen until the bell rang and class was dismissed.

As I waited in the carpool line for my mom, I thought about how often people said I was the spitting image of her—long dark hair, almond-shaped gray eyes, and pale complexion. They always commented on how pretty she was, so I guess that meant I had to be pretty, too. But I never spent tons of time in front of the mirror or fussing over myself, and while I loved shopping and going to the mall like the other girls, they just didn't seem like the most important things to do on a Saturday afternoon. I much preferred taking Danny down to the beach and tossing a ball for him or watching him dive into the surf and chase the seagulls that he could never catch, which always made me laugh. Lulu spent most of her weekends playing soccer or riding her horse, Soprano, out at stables in Malibu, so it was usually Kate who called on the weekend about going to the mall. It was becoming more and more obvious to me that we were starting to have less and less in common.

"Kate talks about herself all the time, Mom. It's starting to drive me and Lulu crazy."

"You've been friends since you were five, Bree, honey," my mom said as we drove off in her SUV.

"I know, Mom, but we're just so different now."

Danny was with her, as he often was when she picked me up from school, all jumpy and tail-wagging happy when he spotted me standing in the carpool line. He leaned over me from the backseat with his panting doggy breath and I grabbed on to his collar to pull him close for a hug. My fingers closed around its worn leather and I realized it was time for a new collar, since he'd been wearing the same one for at least two years.

"Danny needs a new collar, Mom," I said, but she didn't hear me. She was prattling on about how Kate and I would be just fine and how this was just a phase we were going through.

As my mom opened the gate at the bottom of our house with a remote and we pulled in to the driveway, I felt my stomach tighten again, and it wasn't because of Kate or Ashton. Something else was bothering me that I couldn't quite put my finger on. Danny jumped out of the backseat when I held the car door open for him and ran ahead toward the front door. When he got there he sat and looked at me and gave a small woof, which meant, "C'mon, we've got things to do inside."

"Okay, Danny-O, I'm right behind you!" I shouted as I felt my body tense. As I walked up the stairs toward him, another vocab word for the week came to me and I realized it described perfectly what I felt in that moment.

Trepidation: a nervous feeling of uncertainty.

Chapter Three

It was Tuesday, May 15, at 10:23 A.M. when everything in my life changed.

At 10:19 A.M. Mr. Drollinger, our science teacher, was explaining to the class what a hypothesis was. This was for the benefit of a science experiment with tomato seeds, but I never got to do the experiment with the rest of the class. As we were about to begin, a lanky-looking girl arrived with a note from the school secretary that said to go to the office because there was an urgent phone call for me. Lulu wanted to come with me, but Mr. Drollinger said that wouldn't be necessary, so I ran-walked after the messenger girl with skinny, round shoulders as we headed in the direction of the school office. My hands were clammy and cold, and I could feel my heart beating fast all through my body like a hummingbird bashing against a glass house. I felt scared enough to break.

I imagined the worst. A car accident. Mom. Grabbing her laptop, racing down the stairs, high heels screeching against the just-polished wooden floor, cell phone ringing, SUV alarm blaring as she backed out of the driveway to get to the News Story of the Moment . . . except this time she didn't get there.

Or Dad. A plane crash in some remote part of the world where terrorists were hiding out or a war had just erupted and he'd gotten caught in the cross fire. In my panic I couldn't remember if he was in India, the Congo, or Iraq. I flashed back to the moment when he left, my dad giving me a quick kiss while the world was still dark outside and whispering his usual "Bye, kiddo, be back in a jiff" against my hair. "A jiff" was his way of saying a week or two, sometimes even longer.

When I got to the office, the secretary said my mom was on the phone and pointed to a small private area where the Xerox machine and coffee maker were kept.

I took in a deep, ragged breath and picked up the receiver.

"Mom? Are you okay? What about Dad?"

"Fine, we're fine. . . ." She stumbled over the words fast.

"Then what's wrong? I was worried sick."

"Bree, listen, do you have Danny?"

"No. I don't have him. Dogs aren't allowed at school, you know that."

She paused.

"Why are you asking?" I felt suddenly queasy.

"I hoped . . . I've looked everywhere, and I mean everywhere. Bree, he's missing."

"What?" I felt weak and shaky and wanted to sit down but there wasn't a chair.

"Bree, honey," my mom said slowly, "I forgot to close the gate."

"You didn't. You couldn't have. You never . . ." I must have raised my voice, because the school secretary put her head into the room.

"I made a terrible, horrible mistake." She could barely get the last words out. "He's gone."

The air around me felt like it had been sucked out of the room.

"I've got to find him. Come get me now, Mom.

Please!" I gasped like a fish flip-flopping on the ground.

My ocean was my dog. Without him I couldn't breathe.

On the car ride home I sat-lay, half sliding down in the seat because my whole body felt like it had lost its shape and form. In halting sentences my mom told me what had happened.

She had been rushing to cover a story about contaminated pet food that needed to be pulled off the shelves of local supermarkets before any more animals got sick or died, and she forgot to hit the "close" button on the automatic gates to our home. What seemed so unbelievable about the situation was that by trying to save the lives of other dogs, my mom had failed to keep safe the most important pooch of all—Danny.

"It's always your work that comes first, Mom."

"It's not true, honey, you do."

"No, Mom, look, you just lost my dog. It's because of your job that he's gone."

"No, it's because I was careless and rushing. . . ."

"You are always rushing."

"I'm sorry."

"Sorry won't bring him back."

We were silent for the rest of the ride home.

* * *

"Danny! Danny-O!" I shouted as I ran frantically from room to room looking for him. I willed him to be burrowed in my comforter and my mom had just missed checking there. But when I ripped back the covers there was nothing there but a rawhide bone that he must have "buried" in the sheets last night while I slept. I raced through the backyard praying that I'd find him sleeping in the bushes in the far back corner by the lemon tree, as he sometimes did, but after getting on my hands and knees in the dirt and poking my head through the bramble, I saw nothing but leaves and fallen, rotting lemons.

"Danny!" I shouted as I ran down the driveway to the front gate and out onto our street. My mom had taken off in her car to drive the neighborhood to see if she could spot him somewhere.

"I'll find him. Hopefully he hasn't gone too far." Her face looked drawn and paler than usual, and her voice didn't sound very convincing.

I just nodded. I was beyond being able to find words to say to her.

I ran up and down at least twenty streets and back alleys shouting his name and stopping people who walked by. "Please, have you seen a black and white dog; his name's Danny?" I was out of breath and burning hot and my eyes stung sharper with every shake of their heads. I wanted my dad really badly, to tell me it was going to be all right in his calming, warm voice, but he was a million miles away.

I ran into stores on Montana Avenue, which was close to our house, interrupting customers and salespeople with my out-of-breath plea. "Please, have you seen my dog?" But they all just looked at me and shook their heads.

My feet ached and I was parched by the time my mom found me sitting on the side of the road outside our house.

She rolled down the car window. "No luck?"

I kept my eyes focused on the ground and didn't look up. How could I explain to her what she had done to me? How many ways could I say that being so caught up in her job had taken away the one thing that mattered most to me?

"I'm so sorry, Bree. I don't know what to say. . . . Come inside. You look awful."

I shook my head. I sat on the sidewalk until the sun went down and the air got cool. My mom came out at some point with some water and a sandwich for me, but I couldn't eat. I willed the image of Danny, running up our road toward me, his tail wagging, a "hey, a little adventure never hurt anyone, and I'm home now" look on his sweet face, and I scolded him for taking off.

But as the sky turned dark and the street got so quiet that the only sounds were the occasional car going by and chirping crickets, I knew that he wasn't coming back tonight.

Hypothesis. If A = Mom did not have to leave in such a hurry and forget to close the gate, then B would not have happened. B = Danny getting out and running away. A therefore caused B.

B could not have occurred without A.

Chapter Four

My room was painted pale lavender. The decorator had told my mother it was a soothing color, but it didn't help at all. Everything around me looked gray, the colors drained from the walls. I didn't want to talk to anyone, least of all my mom right now, so I did something I never usually did, which was lock my bedroom door.

"Bree, open up! Please." The newsmom knocked softly. "Listen, I feel terrible about this." I could hear her blow her nose and sniffle.

I pulled my knees up close against my chest and let my long dark hair fall over them like a curtain.

"I've made flyers. We'll put them everywhere. I'm offering a big reward for Danny. We'll go to the local shelter tomorrow. I've called everyone we know to come and help us find him." I could hear her French manicured nails raking softly against the door. "C'mon, Bree. I'm doing everything I possibly can to get him back."

"I just want to be left alone. Okay, Mom?" I croaked softly. My voice was practically gone from shouting Danny's name over and over again for hours.

She must have heard me, because after a few seconds I heard her heels click-clicking away.

In the Third Grade Spring Recital I had been a drone bee, not the queen bee, but still, I had to sing the buzzing song and fly around the stage and sing the Bee Happy Bee-cause song that we'd worked on. Just like every other bee in the bunch, I had expected my mom to be there and she promised she wouldn't miss it for anything. But on the day of the recital, there was a huge traffic jam downtown because of a broken water pipe and she had to cover the story. So there I was with my arms flap-flapping, trying hard to make the buzzing sound as tears whooshed their way through my black makeup. I didn't do a good job singing the Bee Happy song, because every other mom was in the school auditorium, smiling and clapping for her bee-utiful daughter. Just not mine.

"I'll make it up to you. Promise. Big, big promise!" my mom said later that night.

Third grade, fourth grade, sixth grade, and now. I couldn't even count how many times she came late to pick me up from drama club, birthday parties, and friends' houses. Her SUV screeching to a halt, passenger door flung open, cell phone in her hand, "I'm so sorry, honey" as she tried to kiss me on the cheek. Puffy, hot red splotches on my face as she prattled on about the disaster, the big event, the sighting, the interview, or whatever it was that had kept her.

Colleen Davies. News reporter first. Mom second.

While she went on and on, I'd go to a brighter place inside to block her out. A fairy princess dress that I'd worn on Halloween, a slice of velvet-soft cake, a piece of lined paper where "A+ and Excellent Work!" was written on the top of my English essay. But once Danny was in my life, I'd mostly close my eyes and see the wagging tail, lick-loving face, softest fur to wrap my wounds around.

I text messaged Kate and Lulu to tell them the news.

Lulu wrote back immediately. *Don't worry, we'll find him!*

I can't believe it. You must be totally mad at your

mom, Kate replied ten minutes later.

The truth was I wasn't mad at my mom. I was devastated.

Out of habit I wiggled my toes near the bottom of my bed, expecting to feel soft fur. That was Danny's spot, curled up like a big pretzel at my feet. I remembered reading somewhere that when a person lost an arm or a leg they could still feel it even though it might have been gone for days or even months. I could still feel Danny's shaggy shape between my raw, blistered toes, like he'd never left.

I thought about how there should be a product called Brain Bottles, with a TV advertisement that came at you in a loud, booming voice and said something like, "Introducing a state-of-the-art new product called Brain Bottles, where all your not-to-be-forgotten great moments in your life are saved forever. The beauty in Brain Bottle storage is that all you have to do is uncork the bottle and take a long, hard whiff and, whammo, you're back in that time of bliss again. Only $19.99 for a set of six."

As I lay on my bed, the Brain Bottle that I wanted to uncork was a warm afternoon last summer.

I'm floating in sparkling blue water. I can smell the tangy chlorine in the pool. My dad's got the camera focused tight on me and Danny splashing around in our backyard pool. I'm laughing, hamming it up for the camera, doing the doggy paddle next to Danny, who's a big boy of three and a half. We're treading water, side by side. I can feel his legs kicking hard against mine and cold licks on my shoulder as I put my arms under his belly and guide him out of the water. Then the sound of my bikini-clad mom shrieking when Danny shakes himself off on the burnished bricks and gets her all wet. The sight of my lean, muscled dad leaning over him and rubbing him dry with his towel, his voice deep and warm. "You big silly goof." I look over at the three of them—Mom, Dad, and Danny—and climb out of the water so I can join them. A sunny, swimming Sunday. Bottled Bliss.

Our family. Together.

Chapter Five

I was walking with Kate and Lulu between classes, and I was having a hard time concentrating on anything at school. With my dad away, me barely talking to my mom, and my fear that I'd never see Danny again, I was in a serious funk.

Kate zigzagged around me. "You need a shiatsu massage. That's what my mom does to relieve her stress."

"No, thanks," I said.

Lulu put her arm around my slumped shoulders. "Think positive, Bree. Danny will come back. I know he will." Her thick mop of dark hair bobbed up and down as she spoke.

"If it was my mom and she lost something really valuable of mine I'd never forgive her," Kate said.

"Being mad isn't going to get him back," Lulu said in her usual practical wisdom kind of way.

"I just saw the cutest puppies at the pet store on Wilshire. They're right by my mom's electrologist. You should get one," Kate suggested.

"There was just a story on TV about how you shouldn't get a puppy from a pet store," Lulu chimed in. "It said you should go to a shelter or something instead."

"It doesn't matter," I said. "Danny's not an object I can just replace."

"Jeez, Bree, it was only a suggestion." Kate tossed her recently highlighted hair in my direction. "I was only trying to help."

"It's okay," I said. "You wouldn't understand. You've never had a pet."

"My parents don't want anything ruining our house," Kate said.

The warning bell rang, and as Kate walked off to her next class I actually felt sorry for her for having parents who cared about the wrong things.

As we got to Miss Jenson's English class, Lulu turned to me. "Look, I know how you feel. I've had dogs all my life."

"When my mom gets back from work, we're going to the Santa Monica shelter to see if he's there. I hope."

Hope was what I needed to get me through the rest of the day.

Since my mom was still at work, I took the school bus home. Once we reached Santa Monica, I craned my neck out of the school bus window and down every street to see if I could spot Danny. No luck.

When I got into the house I decided to make a list of possible scenarios about where Danny might be.

1. Lost, hungry, cold, and scared to let anyone get near him. (Except Danny went up to anyone, being the lovable loverboy that he was.)
2. Trapped under a house being built or in something that he couldn't get out of. (But there wasn't construction going on on our street and he was too smart to go into a small and dark place and get stuck.)
3. Kidnapped by bad and scary men. (But no one had called us asking for ransom money.)
4. Dead. (The hardest one of all to write. My hand felt weak and my handwriting went wiggly on the word.) Killed by a car and lying in a ditch somewhere. (But if someone found a dead dog in

our neighborhood no one would just leave him there. Even if they wouldn't touch him they'd call Animal something-or-other to get him. Right?)

He always wore a brown leather collar that had his name and our address and phone number on it, and I imagined that if someone had found him surely they would have called by now.

I had tons of homework to do, but since Danny's disappearance, focusing on anything else seemed nearly impossible. To make matters worse, I had a "date" with Ashton Adams, which was the last thing I needed during this week of critical calamity.

The phone rang and I put my list down and picked up the purple phone on my bedside table. It was my dad.

"Daddy, where are you?"

"Washington."

"Oh, I thought you were overseas."

"I was. Now I'm here, working on a national political story for a change."

"Come home!" I begged. "Please, Dad. Danny's gone!"

"I know, kiddo, and I'm as sad as you are." He cleared his throat. "Devastated for you, actually. I know what he meant to you. . . ."

"Means to me. Don't say it like he's gone for good."

"I'll try to come home in a few days, Bree."

"But I need you sooner," I said louder. "Please, Dad."

"Okay, I'll do my very best."

I put the phone back in its cradle and wiggled my cold toes against empty air.

Think positive, Bree, I heard Lulu say in my head.

Okay. I would think positive. I would find Danny, no matter what.

"It's on Ninth Street off Olympic Boulevard," my mom said as she drove fast to the shelter. She was, of course, running late coming home, and there were only ten minutes left to get there before they closed at five P.M.

"You promised you'd be home by four, Mom," I said glumly, looking down at my hands.

"I know, honey, but the traffic coming back from the downtown rally that we were covering was horrendous."

"You knew this was important. Why couldn't you be on time?"

"Oh, no, I think I missed the turn!" She did a screeching U-turn and I had to hold on to the car door as we lurched onto Olympic Boulevard. She glanced over at me quickly. "I'm juggling a lot, you know. I'm doing my best."

"But this was—"

"I get it. I said I was sorry."

"No, you don't get it, Mom. You never do." I shook my head.

We made it to the shelter with less than five minutes to spare. It was a small brick building on a cul-de-sac in the more industrial part of Santa Monica. The front doors had posters of a woman with two dogs standing next to her and a cat on her lap. It said VOLUNTEER AT THE SHELTER. HELP YOUR COMMUNITY ANIMALS.

A uniformed female officer looked up at us from behind her desk as soon as we rushed in. She wore a badge that said OFFICER SHEPHERD. What a perfect name for someone who worked with animals. My mom explained quickly to her that we had lost our dog. She handed the flyer of Danny over to the officer and asked if he had been brought in since she last called to check, which had been earlier in the day.

Officer Shepherd looked long and hard at the picture of Danny and shook her head. My mom had used a picture of Danny that stood on the mantelpiece in the living room. It was taken at a picnic that we had last year for my dad's forty-fourth birthday.

"Great lookin' dog. Wish I could say he was brought in. Our shelter's small compared to most, so we remember the face of every dog or cat that comes in or is impounded."

"Can we check, just in case . . . ?" I blurted out.

Officer Shepherd looked up at the clock on the wall. The hands were clearly at five o'clock. "Too late now, young lady, but I promise you, he's not here. I'll post the flyer, though." She stood up and walked toward a corkboard where there were pictures of other lost or missing pets. "You should come back and help out sometime. We're always looking for new young volunteers."

"Thank you for your time," my mother said as we headed out the door, her voice filled with frustration.

There was no point in reminding her that had she been on time we could have at least looked through the shelter ourselves, just to be sure. For once we seemed to be in the same frame of mind. Upset and disappointed.

Chapter Six

I barely slept all night. I kept waking up expecting to hear a familiar bark outside announcing that Danny's little runaway-from-home adventure was over and he was back. But all I heard were trees rustling and an occasional car passing by on our street. It seemed like my mom wasn't sleeping much either, because the hall light kept going on and off and I heard her stop outside my room a few times during the night. I had a split-second twinge of wanting to call to her and have her sit on my bed with her thin, pale arms around me. (She never went in the sun if she could help it because a tan "makes you look dirty on camera," as she always told me.) But the wanting of her company was quickly outweighed by the heavy gray lump in my stomach where all my sadness was collecting, like a giant stratus cloud that would surely burst and drown me if Danny didn't come back soon.

Ashton Adams lived in a big Mediterranean villa in Brentwood that looked like a five-star hotel. It had huge, high walls around it and was gated and guarded like Fort Knox. The drive to his house had been uncomfortable, with my mom trying to make conversation and me mumbling incoherent answers. As much as I was dreading spending the afternoon at Ashton's, I was relieved when our car was buzzed in and the giant, wrought iron gates, with a huge "A" emblem on them, swung open.

Ashton's housekeeper, dressed in a starched, salmon-colored uniform that seemed perfectly coordinated with all the terra-cotta tiles and matching oversized potted plants in the huge entrance hall, smiled and led me into a den. Ashton was lying slouched in a leather couch with his feet up on a marble coffee table, engrossed in what looked like a dangerous mountain climbing snow expedition that was playing on a flat-screen TV that filled an entire wall. I shivered.

"I didn't even hear you come in, Bree." He clicked

off the TV. "Guess we should go rehearse." He sighed as he stretched and stood. I decided it was a signature sound that came out of him whenever the word "Bree" was involved.

I followed him into what turned out to be his father's at-home office. It was like stepping into a "who's who" in showbiz extravaganza. Covering just about every inch of wall space were photographs of Alan Adams—Ashton's dad—posing with major movie stars. His white capped teeth gleamed almost as brightly as the three gold Oscar statuettes that were strategically mounted in a chrome and glass case on the wall behind his huge, mahogany wood desk. I recognized the wood as mahogany because my dad had bought my mom a much smaller mahogany desk when she announced last year that she wanted to do her story research from home instead of at the network so she could be around more. She had never used it except as a place to throw designer jackets and pants that needed altering and glossy magazines that she subscribed to but rarely read.

I looked over at Ashton's father's desk. I gave it high marks for neatness, but that was probably the housekeeper's doing. All it had on it was a laptop, a pile of scripts, and an oversized picture of himself—Mr. Powerful and Famous Movie Director—and a very pretty young blond woman, who was the only person in the pictures

I didn't recognize as someone whose face had been on a billboard on the Sunset Strip in Hollywood.

Ashton sat down in his father's leather chair and faced me like I was there for an audition. He looked right at me with his hazel eyes, a sour look on his otherwise perfect face. I wished I was back in my mother's SUV, tension and all, rather than here in the Hollywood Hall of Fame with a boy who clearly had no interest in being here with me. Turns out that look was meant for someone who had died over four hundred years ago.

"Shakespeare. Ugh. Bo-oring. . . ." He made a face again.

"Depends how you look at it." I sat down in the chair across from him. "His plays have all the same stuff in them as films today."

"Like what?" Ashton challenged me.

I squirmed in my seat under his intense stare. Being ignored by him suddenly felt like a welcome alternative, but I had argued this very issue with my dad not that long ago and felt sure about what I would say next.

"Murder, violence, love, power, comedy. Do those sound familiar?"

Ashton stared at me for what seemed like a long time.

"You're a brain. You get only As in class, right?"

"No, not lately," I answered. I was wearing a new

pair of flats and my feet felt like they were swelling like dough rolls in the oven, as if they needed to be free of the confining shoes and the look on Ashton's face.

"Why not lately?" He picked up the picture of his dad and the pretty blonde and turned it facedown on the desk with a smack.

"My dog ran away a few days ago and I'm having a hard time concentrating in class and I'm scared he won't come back," I blurted out in one long sentence without taking a breath.

"Man, that's the worst," Ashton said, shaking his head.

"I keep imagining he'll show up any minute, but it hasn't happened yet," I said softly.

Ashton stood up suddenly and walked to the office door that lead to the huge expanse of gardens and let out a shrill whistle.

"Buster, Bullwinkle!" he yelled. "Come to Papa-son!"

There was a low, guttural bark, followed by another that got closer and closer, and then they were jumping on him, fat paws pulling, flat noses snorting, and wide jaws slobbering, their short, fat tails wagging. It was an attack of the best kind. Dog licks and jumps that had Ashton falling on the floor with them. A rolling around together of tails and tongues and legs and arms.

"Meet the bulldogs from hell!" Ashton laughed as they pinned him down.

The smiling, salmon-uniformed housekeeper suddenly appeared at the study door. She wasn't smiling anymore. "Your daddy say no doggy in his office!" she scolded Ashton in her broken English.

"Okay, okay, Consuela. Don't look so mad." He got to his feet and punched her lightly on the arm and gave her a big white-toothed smile. I watched as she melted, like butter in a microwave. Zap, zap, zap.

"You take the doggies out from here, okay, chico? Me no say nothing to your daddy." She patted Ashton's arm affectionately before leaving.

Buster and Bullwinkle had since discovered me in the chair and were trying to sniff every inch of me. I realized that the last time I had worn these jeans I had been lying on the couch in the den watching TV with Danny, who had been pressed up close and snuggly in front of me. Ashton's bulldogs could clearly smell him on me.

"We should rehearse," I said, feeling suddenly sorry for myself. Ashton had a perfect life, a perfect smile, and two perfectly safe dogs, slobber and all.

"I'm really sorry your dog's gone. I mean, if anything happened to these two . . ." He leaned close to me and hugged their big heads. "I'd be totally out-of-my-mind crazy."

"What do you mean?" I said with surprise.

Ashton walked over and sat down behind his father's big desk again.

"The parents had a nasty divorce a year ago. My mom moved to New York. I haven't seen her in almost five months. And Dad"—he picked up the photograph that was facedown and held it up—"is about to marry *her.*" He jabbed his finger at the young blonde's face. "Yeah, wannabe actress and half his age."

"Wow, I had no idea. . . ."

"Yeah, no idea about anything is what soon-to-be stepmonster Stephanie is all about. The only thing she knows for sure is that she doesn't like me. Or my dogs." He shook his head. "I worry that once they're married I'll come home from school and they'll be gone. Like she'll take them and dump them somewhere."

"She wouldn't!" I said.

"Nah, Consuela's been our housekeeper since I was three. She's my dog guard, or guard dog, if you know what I mean." He put the photograph of his father and his fiancée back down on the desk facing the right way up and sighed. I knew it wasn't meant for me. "But I still wouldn't put anything past Stephanie."

"I'm sorry, really, I am."

Ashton coughed and cleared his throat. "What's your dog's name?"

"Danny." The sound of his name spoken in this unfamiliar place made me miss him even more. At home I could still picture him, his shiny silver bowls engraved with the words "food" and "water" still waiting to be filled in the kitchen. His big downy doggy bed still left with the imprint that his body had last made. At home I could still hold on to the fact that Danny still was. But out in the world there were no markers for me to run my fingers over to remind me that he still existed.

"I've had him since he was a puppy," I said quietly.

"Yeah, I got Buster and Bullwinkle when they were ten weeks old. They're brothers, from the same litter."

"That's lucky. They've always had each other . . . and you," I said.

"And Danny's always had you," Ashton added.

"I guess I just expected he'd always be around. I never thought something like this would ever happen."

"It's horrible." Ashton shook his head.

"I was at the Santa Monica Shelter yesterday hoping he'd be there, but he wasn't." I sighed. "You know, I just realized, I'm not the only one. There are other dogs and other owners who are missing their pets, too. I want to help them."

Ashton looked at me. I mean, really looked at me in a way that made me want to turn away, but I didn't.

"That's cool, Bree." He smiled. "Thinking about

other people when you're dealing with your own lost pet."

"Thanks." I blushed.

"Listen, if you like, I'll help you find Danny. No sweat."

"Really?"

"Yeah, really. Dog lovers have to stick together, don't they?"

Chapter Seven

I was anxious to speak to my mother on the ride home from Ashton's. I wanted to tell her about Buster and Bullwinkle and Ashton's wicked soon-to-be stepmother, but most importantly, I wanted to share with her that the most popular boy in seventh grade was going to help me find Danny.

But at 6:30 P.M., which was the time we had agreed for her to come, she didn't show up. My cell phone, which I'd put on vibrate while we were rehearsing, buzzed in my pocket. I assumed it was a message from my mom, calling to say she had been let through the "A" gates and was waiting for me like a dutiful mother in the circular driveway. But she wasn't.

"So sorry, honey, but the station needs me to cover a bear attack in the Angeles National Forest. I'm racing over there as fast as . . . No, Larry! The 210 freeway, not the 405!" she yelled suddenly. "Sorry, the cameraman's driving us there. Anyway, I'm sure there's someone in that enormous house who can give you a ride home. Far left lane, Larry! Yes . . . left! Don't be mad, Bree. Please, okay. I'll make it u—" I hit delete without waiting to hear the rest.

The family driver was out running errands, so Ashton got Consuela to drive me home in her old car. She insisted that I sit in the backseat, but I refused. I was embarrassed enough by the whole ordeal and didn't want Consuela to think I expected her to act like a chauffeur. I must have said "muchos gracias" a thousand times to her for driving me. On the way Consuela filled me in on how bad everything was for Ashton since his parents had split up. She said she was glad that he had such a nice friend like me and that I must come over a lot because "he is very sore in his heart now."

"But Ashton has tons of friends," I told Consuela as we pulled up outside our two-story house.

"Si, he has lots of amigos to laugh with." She turned the ignition off and her car came to a muttering stop. "But is all like play you rehearse. Is act." She turned to look at me with her warm, liquid eyes. "He is, I see, different with you. Is because, I feel, you are a little sad, too. Yes?"

I drummed my fingers on the cover of my copy of *A Midsummer Night's Dream* in my lap and nodded.

Consuela made a clucking noise with her tongue. "Is parents also divorce?"

I shook my head. They were together, just never around, I wanted to say, but didn't.

"Good news! Somebody stay married in this crazy city." She slapped her hands on the torn leather steering wheel as if everything were suddenly solved. "In my country we stay together. No thinking to divorce, even if one is working many years in America and one is still in Guatemala and not possible to see each other very much."

I wondered if Consuela's husband and family missed her a lot since she had lived with Ashton's family for so long, but I didn't want to seem nosy and ask her.

"You be happy girl now." She smiled and patted my arm as I got out of the car.

"Thanks again, Consuela," I said, then turned and walked toward the empty house.

I was planning on calling Lulu immediately to fill her in on the afternoon's turn of events with Ashton, but when I picked up my bedroom phone to call, the triple beep let me know that there were three messages waiting. The first was from the newsmom letting me know that she was rushing so she didn't have time to write a note, but that there were chicken and a salad in the fridge for dinner and she'd be home by nine. The second call was from Kate's mother. She wanted to tell me that she wouldn't be sending out invitations to Kate's birthday party because there wasn't time, but ten of us would be spending the day at a spa getting "the whole shebang," whatever that meant. The third message was from a person whose voice I didn't recognize.

"Hi, my name is Martha Stein. I hope someone will get this. You see, I was pruning the outside hedges"—her voice was slow and halting—"and I found a collar, a dog's collar, I believe, with your phone number and address, so I'm calling right away."

I felt the whole room tilt and my heart drop like it was speeding downhill on a roller coaster.

"Yes, Danny, it says right here," the woman continued. "Well, I do hope that someone gets this message. I'll be home all evening, so feel free to come by. I live at 1293 Marguerita Avenue. A yellow house with white trim; you can't miss it."

I had kicked off my shoes when I got home and

didn't even wait to put them on again. I ran barefoot out the front door, down the driveway, and onto the street in the direction of Marguerita Avenue. Within the space of the few minutes it took for me to get there, a hundred thoughts raced through my nervous, excited, jumbled brain. As I sprinted through an intersection at Fourth Street and made a quick left onto Marguerita, I had to believe that, surely, if there was a collar, there must be a dog not too far behind.

I rang the doorbell of the white-shuttered house with rows of daffodils leading up the pathway to the front door. I was completely out of breath, more from anxiety than the jog over.

A small gray-haired woman opened the door.

"I'm Bree Davies." I sucked in air. "I just got your message, about the dog, I mean, dog collar."

She looked me over with kind, watery blue eyes and took in my naked feet.

"You must have been in an awful hurry to get it back." She smiled and held the door open for me.

I followed her through her quaint house filled with vases of brightly colored flowers and hand-stitched lace cloths that covered every surface. She opened a drawer in her immaculate kitchen and handed me the painfully familiar, worn, brown leather collar. The sight of it made me feel hopeful and crushed all at once. She held it out to me and I took it slowly from her. I ran my fingers over it and I noticed that a few of Danny's soft hairs clung to the inside. Then I saw that at its most worn spot it had snapped.

"Oh, no!" I said. "It broke and came off his neck!"

"Oh, I am sorry," the woman said. "I just realized. The flyers that are posted everywhere. It's your dog that's gone missing."

"Can you show me where you found it?" I looked up from the dog collar at her.

"Why, yes. Of course. Can I offer you a glass of water? You look a little ashen." Her thin mouth puckered at the corners.

"No. Don't worry. I'm fine."

I followed her through the back gate into the alley, where a wheelbarrow overflowing with chopped-off leaves still stood.

"I was pruning. The hedges grow high awfully fast, and no one has trimmed them since my husband passed away." She looked up at her handiwork. "Tim was an excellent gardener, you see, kept the yard pristine. I'm afraid I don't have his green thumb." She shook her head.

"Your garden is beautiful, Mrs. . . . ?"

"Martha. Call me Martha. And you're Bree, is that right?"

I nodded. "I'm sorry about your husband."

"And I'm sorry about your dog." The sun was just starting to cast streaks of gold and orange ribbons across the sky as Martha and I faced each other in the early evening light. "I know how hard it is to be without someone you love. I see how much your dog means to you."

"How do you know?" I asked.

"By the way you ran your fingers over his collar. Touch tells us so much."

Martha showed me the place in the bushes where she had found Danny's collar.

I tried to imagine him sniffing the hedges and lifting his leg to mark the spot as his own, like he always did when I walked him. "You, Danny-O, think you own the whole neighborhood!" I would tell him as he lifted his leg on a wall or a tree base for the umpteenth time on a walk. "You know, some bigger dog is going to follow right behind you and claim the territory as his." But Danny would just wag his tail and give me a big happy grin and keep on doing the thing that came naturally to him and all boy dogs, I guessed.

I thanked Martha for calling and offered to come

and help her with the hedges if she needed.

"That's very sweet of you, Bree. But sooner or later I'm going to have to get used to taking care of things on my own." She picked up the wheelbarrow handles in her frail hands. "I was very lucky to have a wonderful husband like Tim, but I'm afraid he took care of most things, which has left me with lots to learn to do for myself now."

I held the gate open for Martha and watched as she carefully made her way back into the garden that she had, I imagined, enjoyed with her husband for many, many years.

"Thank you!" I yelled through the fence.

"Stay in touch!" she shouted back. "I'll say a special prayer tonight."

I held Danny's collar tightly in my hand and called his name over and over again as I made my way down the alley. I willed him to hear me, wherever he was. I told him that I was just as lost without him as he was right then and that I needed him back. Even though the light was fading fast now, I kept going. My bare feet were cold and the undersides cut from the sharp, biting gravel.

"DANNY!" I screamed, his name echoing back to me in the silent alley.

Then, out of the corner of my eye, I saw a dark, four-legged animal dart behind some large trash cans. I picked up my pace and shouted Danny's name again. The animal took off. It was a dog; I could tell by the size and the gait. It was dark in shadows now, so I couldn't make out the markings or color, but I was sure, as I had never been before, that it had to be, must be, could not be anyone, anything, but Danny.

I ran like I had never run before to catch him.

Chapter Eight

The dog ducked and darted down the alley and then kept going without stopping. I was gaining ground. Having been on the track team for a few years was now paying off. I remember telling my mother that track was taking up too much of my time right before I quit, but now I was grateful that my body was still in athlete mode, trained endurance. I moved at bullet speed, despite the searing pain in my feet. Catching Danny was all that mattered. I was close enough to see him turn and look back at me, a quick glimpse of white on his chest. My spirits rose. I screamed his name again and, for just a split second, wondered why he wasn't turning around and running toward the voice that loved him most. "DA-AAA-N-Y!"

Just a few yards was all that stood between us now, but the world around me suddenly shifted into slow motion as horror filled my heart.

An expanse of street lay right ahead. Black asphalt, a deadly, dangerous river to cross. Then, a car's headlights. The fast-moving dog galloping out toward it on a collision course with metal that would surely take him from me before I got him back.

"NOOOOO!" I screamed, my feet accelerating at a speed they had never reached before. Then I sprung, high and wide, every muscle in my body focused, like a cheetah onto its prey.

The night air whooshed by me. The screeching sound of brakes, the smell of rubber burning, my thigh hitting hard against the ground, a blast of pain, but beneath me was soft fur and a heart that I could feel beating louder than the car driver who yelled obscenities at me as I lay in the middle of the road with the dog pinned beneath me.

"You stupid girl!" the man bellowed. "Coulda killed you both!"

I didn't move, couldn't lift my head to see the person that suddenly responded to him.

"Damn brilliant, if you ask me. Haven't seen a dog catch like that since Hurricane Katrina. I'm her mom. So sorry, sir!" a woman's voice said.

"Danny," I whispered into his fur as the sky and earth closed dark around me.

"Tell your daughter to be more careful!" the man yelled. I heard the sound of squealing brakes as his car took off.

I knew my feet were bleeding. My leg pulsed with pain. Then I felt someone's hands laced through my bruised fingers and the person pulling me up slowly to sit. "Easy does it," the woman said.

I caught a glimpse of a choke chain and leash in her hands, which she placed carefully over the dog's head. I was dazed. My mom was in the Angeles National Forest covering a story, so who was this woman who had called me her daughter and helped me to the sidewalk, the panting dog on his leash at her heels.

"Mom, Danny," I whispered, the world tilting as I lay my head down.

"No, not Mom, sweet pea. I had to say that to get rid of him. Didn't need an angry man out of his car in the dark." Long, curly hair covered my face.

"Not Mom . . ." I murmured, looking up at her angular chin.

"And not Danny," she said softly. "This here is

Clay." Been trying to catch him all day. Thanks to you, we've got him now."

"Not Danny. It has to be. . . ." I mumbled.

I opened my eyes and looked at Clay, who seemed calm now beside the woman.

She had given him a dog treat and he was gobbling it down fast.

He was black, mostly, with a pointed nose and perked-up ears. How could I have thought he was Danny? Apart from their size and a splash of white on his chest, they looked nothing alike. I felt my head throb and my eyes burn.

"Clay, say thanks to the pretty girl who saved you." The woman rubbed his coat.

"Danny." I barely managed to get out his name. I wanted to tell her that he was my dog and he was missing, but my tongue felt thick and swollen in my mouth.

"He's your dog and he's missing. I know, sweet pea." She moved toward my feet and wrapped them in her sweater. "Let's get you some medical attention. Got a first aid kit in my truck."

I looked at her properly for the first time. She was tall and lean and moved gracefully, like a ballet dancer. She instructed me to put my arms around her neck. I wanted to tell her that there was no way she could carry me and hold on to the dog at the same time, but she lifted me like I weighed nothing. My head was pressed up close against her neck. She smelled of lavender and wet earth, right after a rain. She held me in one strong arm and Clay's leash in her other. When we reached her truck, which was parked in the next alley, she opened the passenger door and carefully lowered me in, then whistled. Clay hopped over me into the driver's seat. I watched him lick her face as she cooed in his ear and secured his leash to the headrest behind.

"You're a bad boy for getting out, but you're not going back. You, Clay-man, are comin' home with me till we find you a better home."

"He's not yours?" I asked as she rummaged in the backseat.

"He's one of my rescue dogs, who I'd placed in a home just a few blocks from here. Nice family, but careless. He got out the day after they adopted him, which was yesterday. In my book that makes them not eligible to get him back. At least they called to tell me right away." She knelt beside me and propped my feet in her lap as she poured something cold and stingy into the cuts then wrapped a gauze bandage around them like she'd done it a thousand times before. As a final touch, she whipped out a pocket knife and snipped and tucked the ends.

"I was up all night trying to find him. Saw the flyers

for your Danny dog, too, and hoped I'd find both of them. I was planning on camping out again straight through the night until you saved the day for Clay."

She held a bottle of something unfamiliar to my lips and made me drink. "'Elixir to fix-er' is what my mama the homeopath always said, may she rest in peace."

The drink tasted like sweet-scented flowers, a flavor I had never imagined before, but it seemed magically to clear my fuzzy, sore head.

"What's your name?" I asked as she moved Clay to the back of the truck and hopped into the driver's seat.

"Rayleen from Savannah, Georgia. You?"

"Bree from around the corner."

She turned to look at me and smiled, her wild, caramel-colored curls bouncing like colliding music notes. There was a large gap between her two front teeth and her startling green eyes were set too far apart, yet she was beautiful in the oddest kind of way.

"Well, Bree from around the corner," she said, and gave me a gaping smile, "which way is home?"

Home. The word sent a dull ache through me.

"Home is on Alta Drive. I'm not sure where we are right now."

"Alta it is." She revved the truck's engine. "I walked this here neighborhood so many times in the past twenty-four hours, it's startin' to feel like I live here myself."

"Where do you live?" I asked

"Topanga Canyon. Way the heck up there. Dirt road and no streetlights, but nobody gets to bother me and my barking pack of mutts."

As she put the truck into reverse, I thought about how angry my parents would be if they knew I'd gotten into a car with a total stranger, a wild-haired dog saver in a truck. As we drove the few short blocks, with country music blaring from the radio and Clay adding an occasional bark, I hoped that when my mother saw my shredded feet, she would understand my taking a ride, just this once, from a woman I had just met.

Later that night I lay on the couch with a bowl of chicken soup that my mom had made for me. I'd had to explain the bandaged feet and what happened while she was out in the Angeles National Forest. I could hear her on the kitchen phone telling my dad, "Yes, Todd, she should have known better, but she couldn't walk, for goodness' sake, and the woman did bring her home safely. Well, then, come back and take charge. She's understandably very upset at the moment about Danny and she got a C on a science test."

"C-plus!" I yelled from my couch position.

She spoke a little longer to my dad, then hung up

the phone and came over to sit on the couch opposite me.

"Bree, your dad says he's sorry it wasn't Danny that you were chasing, but now this woman knows where we live. I covered a story once about a young girl who got a ride home from a strange woman and two weeks later they were robbed. The burglars took everything out of their home that wasn't bolted down." She patted her hair. "This woman might be dangerous, you just never know."

"She saves dogs, Mom." I looked at my mother's not-a-strand-out-of-place cap of dark hair. She was still dressed in her work suit, beige and tasteful.

She gave me a wan smile. "Just glad you're okay, but don't do it again is all I'm asking." She stood up, stretched, and yawned. "Wanna come upstairs and watch TV with me?" she asked.

I shook my head.

"She's taking me to the shelter with her on Saturday," I said as she headed out the door.

My mom stopped in her tracks and turned to me.

"Sorry, Bree, what did you just say?"

"I said Rayleen is picking me up this weekend and taking me with her to an animal shelter where she volunteers. Look, Mom, you're gone all day anyway. Isn't it your weekend to play anchor?" I chose the word that I knew would make her perfect hair stand on edge.

"Not play anchor, Bree, honey. *Be* anchor," my mom said.

I thought about how Rayleen had called me her daughter even though it had only been to get the angry driver who almost hit us to go away. I wanted to tell my mother but didn't. Instead I tried the winning approach.

"Rayleen wants to meet you, Mom. She's seen you on TV and thinks you're gorgeous . . . and so smart," I added just for good measure.

My mother walked back into the room and looked down at me. "Really? How nice of her to say that."

Rayleen, I was sure, didn't have a clue who Colleen Davies was. I doubted that she even watched TV, but I had already gotten myself in too deep. "Yes, that story that you did about the deaf boy who raised money to save his dying brother was her favorite."

"Well, what do you know, someone liked the story."

"I'll make sure she's here before you leave," I added quickly. "She won't be able to sit around and chat, though. She has to get to the shelter. . . ."

My mother agreed that I could go with Rayleen as long as they met first and she could take down her driver's license number. Rayleen had only lived in LA for a few months and probably had an out-of-state license. I hoped she wouldn't mind sharing her personal details with my journalist mom.

Before I went to sleep I prayed that Danny was still alive and safe and that he would soon be back with me.

Chapter Nine

School the next day was not fun. Lulu had taken a fall off Soprano and was resting up at home, so I had to listen to Kate's spa birthday details all by myself.

To add to my bad morning, my English teacher, Miss Jenson, asked me to stay after class so she could discuss my recent book report on *Robinson Crusoe*, on which I had received a stunning C, a grade I had never received before in her class. English was far and away my favorite subject. It must have been a result of all those "reporter" genes passed down to me by the news-parents—at least there was something positive that had come out of their creative hand-me-downs.

"You're an A student, Bree, so what happened here?" Miss Jenson pointed her small chin in my direction with a scowl on her face.

"I'm not sure," I lied. I wanted to get to my next class on time so I wouldn't get the up-and-down stares from everyone as I walked in with a late note.

"Well, if you're not sure, then I can't help you. But this is not up to your usual work." She tapped the typed essay. "Try harder next time, and take more time. This feels rushed and sloppy. Not like you at all." She sighed and shook her salt-and-pepper pixie cut.

I promised Miss Jenson that I would try harder and rushed off to drama lab.

Ashton was seated at the back of the drama lab with an empty chair beside him. After handing Mr. Matheson my late note, I slid into the vacant seat next to him, hoping he would turn and look at me. But he didn't.

Mr. Matheson, who had his hair in a faux Mohawk tinged with purple at the tips today, was reading the role of Helena from *A Midsummer Night's Dream* in a high-pitched voice to a pretend Demetrius, who he had drawn on the chalkboard behind him. The class tittered as his voice went higher and higher in octave.

"I am your spaniel, and, Demetrius,
The more you beat me I will fawn on you.
Use me but as your spaniel: spurn me, strike me,
Neglect me, lose me; only give me leave,
Unworthy as I am, to follow you.
What worser place can I beg in your love—
And yet a place of higher respect with me—
Than to be usèd as you use your dog?

I felt my heart squeeze tight in my chest when the class laughed and applauded as Mr. Matheson walked toward the chalk sketch of Demetrius and curtsied and blew him a kiss.

"Encore!" everyone yelled. It was then, while the rest of our class was distracted, and focused on our pirouetting teacher, that Ashton turned to me. "Jeez, they sure treated dogs badly in Shakespeare's day."

I nodded. What had struck me about the pathetic plea from Helena was not the reference to the ill treatment of the spaniel that was used symbolically but the last line, "Usèd as you use your dog." The words played like a song stuck in its track over and over again in my head. Had I used Danny to fill a void in me, to make me feel better, to keep me from feeling less lonely when the newsparents were gone? Did he somehow sense that he met some need, some requirement? Was he just a replacement? A gap stopper? And worse of all, did he feel all this more than he felt loved by me?

Mr. Matheson wrote an essay topic on the board and everyone jotted it down. It had something to do with why Shakespeare had truly happy endings only among the fairy folk in the play and not among the mortals. I put my head down on my desk for a second, feeling suddenly very tired by the weight of the question.

"Wakey, wakey, Bree." Mr. Matheson rapped a ruler on his desk. Apparently he had asked me a question that I hadn't even heard. I sat up with what must have been a down-turned mouth.

"Uh-oh, why the glum look on your face, Bree?" He walked across the classroom and stood directly in front of me.

"Sorry," I mumbled.

"I asked how rehearsals were going with you and Ashton."

The whole class turned to the back row to look at us.

"Um, fine," Ashton blurted out, since I seemed to have lost my tongue.

"Excellent!" Mr. Matheson gave Ashton a wink. "You're a well-matched king and queen. A very attractive couple." There were snickers followed by laughter from the rest of the class. I slid down as far as I could in my seat.

"Now, now, class." Mr. Matheson frowned and whispered to me that I didn't look very well, and did I need to go to the nurse's office?

I shook my head vigorously. The last thing I needed was to be poked and prodded and put under a microscope by the nosy school nurse.

Thankfully the end-of-period bell rang and we all filed out. Ashton caught up with me as I hurried down the hallway.

"Hey, Bree, wait up!" he said loud enough for everyone close by in the corridor to hear.

I stopped at the sound of my name and turned around. Ashton had his gray sweatshirt hoodie up over his head, but his hazel eyes were focused on me. I noticed that some of the kids from class were watching as Ashton joined me and we continued down the hallway. I figured he probably wanted to talk to me about our next rehearsal, but I was wrong.

"Listen, Bree, I'm sorry if I was a bit weird when you sat down next to me in drama lab, but all my friends are acting so lame about us being the married royalty."

"It's a play. Not real life," I replied.

"Yeah, I know. They're such dorks, and Mr. Matheson and his comments aren't helping any." He shook his head. "But hey, listen, what I wanted to talk to you about was getting together this weekend to create a 'Lost Dog, Big Reward!' website for Danny, and also get more flyers printed to hand out in the neighborhood. I really think it'll help us find him."

The sound of an "us" instead of a "me" finding Danny made my bad day suddenly seem amazingly good. That is, until someone slammed a book bag down on Ashton's head from behind.

"Ouch, moron, that hurt!" Ashton gave his best friend, Max, a punch on the arm.

Skinny, lanky Max laughed and did a big fake bow as the three of us continued down the hallway.

"Sooooo sorry, King Oberon." Max wedged his way in front of us and grabbed my hand and tried to kiss it as he bowed again. "Queen Titania."

I pulled my hand away.

"Knock it off!" Ashton sounded more than irritated.

I said a hasty good-bye without replying to Ashton that yes, getting together on Sunday would be great. I ducked into the science lab, where Mr. Drollinger was setting up what he informed us was a "peanut observation lab."

We each had to select a peanut to "adopt," and then after measuring its girth, width, length, color variations, and noticeable flaws, we had to throw it back into the peanut bin and try to find our very own peanut again using the information that we had written down.

As I held on to my chosen peanut and tried to get to know it very well, I decided that if I could find my peanut again in the bag of nuts, surely I would be able to find my very special dog somewhere in sprawling, huge Los Angeles.

Chapter Ten

"You said she would be here by now, Bree. It's already ten."

The newsmom paced back and forth, her crisp, cream-colored suit snapping to attention as she sliced through the living room while I lounged on one of the couches.

"Leave, then," I told her, knowing that she wouldn't. I picked up a magazine and flipped through it, pretending to seem nonchalant and not at all concerned.

I was dressed in sneakers and my oldest jeans, which is what Rayleen had told me on the phone to wear.

"Messy work. Sometimes smelly, too!" She laughed. "Hope you're up to it." I assured her I would be fine, although the thought of seeing lots of dogs when none of them was Danny was now making me feel queasy. The newsmom's tension tirade wasn't helping the sick feeling that was swirling in my stomach either.

"I think this is a bad idea, Bree. Stay home rather, or call Lulu."

"She's home, resting up, Mom," I quipped.

"Well, do something with Kate, then."

"She's out shopping with her mom." I pulled my knees up to my chest and looked at her. My mom's face was free of makeup and she looked like she was ten years younger. The news station makeup artist would pile on the layers until she looked perfect and polished before she went on camera, but I thought this was her best look, all fresh and clean faced, despite her foul mood.

My mom looked at me and sighed. "You're looking pale and you've lost weight. Drink a protein shake to pick you up."

"I'm not hungry," I said.

She sat down dejectedly on the couch next to me. "I wish more than anything I could undo that day and the gate and everything . . . but I can't. You know I'm not

Cruella Deville." Her eyes started to well up. "I loved Danny. . . ."

The gate phone rang just at that moment and I jumped up to answer it.

"Oh, no!" My mother touched her face. "I'm a mess."

"You're fine, Mom," I said. "It's just Rayleen, not some TV executive."

I was relieved that Rayleen had made it before the newsmom had to leave, otherwise I would have been housebound all day.

"I'm awful sorry I'm late," Rayleen singsonged sweetly, her southern drawl even more pronounced than I remembered it. "I was followin' up on a dog that was found. See, I thought it might be yours, but no luck." She shook her caramel curls and held out a long, muscular arm.

My mother had somehow managed to throw on a fresh coat of red lipstick in the minutes it took for Rayleen to come up our driveway and park. The combination of the newsmom's cream suit, dark hair, and glossy lips was nothing less than dazzling. I could see Rayleen take her in like she was looking at a beautiful, exotic orchid.

"Why, ma'am, what a pleasure." She gave my mom

a gap-toothed smile and shook her manicured hand.

I watched my mom stifle a grimace at the strength of Rayleen's firm grip, but she did it with a smile, like a true professional.

"I can't thank you enough for helping my daughter the other evening. I told her how strangers are often just friends we don't know, and how few truly kind people there are left in this world and surely you must be one of them. . . ."

I wanted to laugh but held myself back. I was waiting to see how diplomatic the newsmom would be in getting Rayleen's drivers' license number after all that mushy praise.

"Well, I know how bad she's hurtin' 'bout her Danny boy. And she saved my Clay, who woulda died under that car if it weren't for Bree."

"Really!" My mother seemed surprised. "I had no idea. . . . We haven't had much time together the past few days, what with my work schedule and her busy school life. . . ."

Rayleen smiled a long, slow smile. "I remember workin' like a crazy woman and bein' nonstop busy. Not my life anymore, no sir. Left that world an' the no-good boyfriend back in New Orleans. Saved a bunch of soggy, starving dogs, rented a huge moving van, and brought 'em all to California after the hurricane. Never went back."

"I covered so much of that terrible situation on air," my mom said.

I watched as Rayleen took in the designer-decorated house and the newsmom, who fit right in. Cream on cream. Silk on silk.

Rayleen wore tan cargo pants and a black tank top that had a Yogic "Om" embroidered in red across its center.

"I used to teach yoga, but my work is rescuing dogs now," she said, as if her life résumé needed completing.

"We'd better be going, Mom. Weren't you worried you'd be late?" I suddenly blurted out, realizing that in a sentence or two Rayleen would probably tell her she had no TV and had never watched the news on Channel Five.

"Oh my! I am very late. Yes, let's." My mom grabbed her briefcase and we all headed to the circular driveway.

"That pretty mama of yours needed the whole deal. Age and license. Expiration date included."

"That's my mom. Charming, competent, and always with an agenda," I groaned as we listened to Elvis and drove on the 10 freeway toward downtown.

"Hey, be grateful you still have her, sweet pea. Mine's gone three years now and I miss her more 'n' more every day. Nothin' like appreciatin' someone when they're gone."

We talked and laughed and sang "Blue Suede Shoes" all the way to downtown, a place I had hardly ever been except to go to the Dorothy Chandler Pavillion when I was seven to see *Peter Pan*. We pulled into the parking lot of a gray, square building. I was in a happier mood than I had been in a while. Rayleen had a calming effect on me.

But as I opened the car door, nothing could have prepared me for the barking and howling of what sounded like hundreds of dogs from inside the shelter walls.

Chapter Eleven

I followed Rayleen in through the double doors. The smell of disinfectant and kennels still needing to be cleaned hit me instantly, and I felt my stomach lurch like a boat on rough seas. I quickly realized that this shelter was very different from the one in Santa Monica. At the entrance was a man with an unshaven face and stooped shoulders. He had a black Lab who was straining against a short leash. The big dog pulled and tugged and whined and reared up like a horse. "Now, stop, Neptune!" The man yanked hard on the dog's collar. "Gotta leave you here, buddy. No home to go back to anymore. Can only feed one mouth." The dog must have sensed that something was terribly wrong because he let out a loud howl that blended in with the noise of all the dogs who were already inside the shelter.

Rayleen quickly went over to help.

I watched as she leaned closer to the confused dog and whispered words to get him to relax. She rubbed her hand up and down his smooth coat. "It's gonna be all right. It's okay, big boy."

Neptune looked at her with big anxious eyes. "I've got him," she told the man. He handed her the leash without blinking. Rayleen was wearing a shelter badge and had given me a volunteer badge to wear in the car. I felt its hard edges dig against my heart as I placed my hand instinctively over it.

Neptune seemed to quiet down at Rayleen's touch, and the scruffy-looking man moved forward to the Animal Control Officer, who was dressed in an official blue uniform and was sitting on the other side of a glass-paneled divider. His badge said his name was Officer Reyes. He barely looked up, but I heard him say "Relinquish or Stray?" to the man in a monotone voice, like he'd said those words a thousand times before, almost in the same way a tired waitress in a diner might ask a patron if they wanted cream and sugar in their coffee.

Relinquish was a vocab word I knew well. I

remembered it from our pop quiz about six months ago. Relinquish. To give up. To withdraw or retreat from. To leave behind.

I felt sick inside as the man mumbled, "Relinquish," and handed over the five dollars he had to pay to leave his dog and walk away, which he did without looking back.

The black Lab strained on his leash as he watched his owner shuffle on torn tennis shoes out the door. He let out a yelp as the door smacked shut, and Rayleen hushed him again with sweet words. I realized in that moment that what was extraordinary, amazing, and above all, heartbreaking about dogs was that they loved unconditionally and with every inch of their beings. They loved owners who beat them, starved them, neglected them in backyards, kicked them, left them in the rain without shelter, and yes, abandoned them. Neptune was no different than any other dog. He wanted his owner back at any cost. He loved him and didn't understand why his owner had let his doggy world fall apart. I let out a ragged sigh and shook my head.

"You okay, sweet pea?" Rayleen asked as she slipped Neptune's collar off and tossed it into a large metal bin. I flinched when I saw that it was full almost to the top with collars in all fabrics and sizes. They had once belonged to dogs whose owners had secured them to their necks. "Relinquish or stray" echoed through my head.

Rayleen placed a simple blue noose on Neptune's neck and he held still while she looked deeply into his eyes. "Your old man cared. Just not enough to fight to keep you." Neptune looked forlornly at her, as if he understood.

"What'll happen now?" I almost had to yell against a sudden rise in the din of dogs.

"He'll be given an impound number and put in a cage with a few other dogs of similar size. He'll go on the shelter website and hopefully some nice person will come and adopt him and he'll have a happy ending." I followed as Rayleen opened a door and led Neptune through. The howling and barking were even louder in here. Rayleen waved to a few other volunteers who were bathing some little dogs in a side room.

"Later I'll introduce you to the New Hope coordinator."

"What's New Hope?" I asked.

"Red listed dogs. I'll explain after I give this handsome boy over." She patted Neptune on the head.

Rayleen handed Neptune over to Officer Reyes, who didn't even look at him but led him to a holding cage, then went back to his desk to fill out his paperwork. In less than five minutes Neptune went from having an owner to having none, and from having a name to being called by a number. Like jail. Except he hadn't committed a crime. I thought how fitting it was that he was named after a planet. Poor Neptune's fate was in his unlucky stars, which had given him the wrong human as his owner.

"People need to know about this place!" I wanted to say to Rayleen. Here was a world so far away from anything I had known before. No one in my school could even imagine a place like this existed. Dingy, smelly, and full of sadness.

I felt sick about Danny. For all I knew he had been dumped at a shelter far away and was just a number now as well. While I helped Rayleen get water buckets and containers of food to distribute from the back kitchen, she told me that "red listed" meant dogs whose time was up.

"Meaning what?" I asked, straining to carry a giant bag of dog food down the hallway.

"Meaning euthanized, sweet pea. Put to sleep 'cause no one wanted them."

I practically dropped the bag on the concrete floor. "I thought they came here to be safe. Isn't this place called a 'shelter'?"

Rayleen tossed her curls back. "Yes, but some shelters get full, with no room for the new animals coming in."

"How long does it take before an animal is in danger?"

Rayleen stood in front of the huge double doors that led to the area of caged kennels. She turned to look at me, her wide-set green eyes locked on mine. "Five days is the law. Sometimes longer. Listen, sweet pea, that's why when you walk through these doors and meet the pups that are here, you've gotta give each one all the love you have in your heart. So when they leave, either to go to a home or to the doggy heaven above, what they remember from this place is kindness and caring. A soft touch, a gentle voice. Okay?"

"Okay," I said in a wavering voice.

"You can do this. Remember, you're the brave gal who threw herself in front of a car to save a dog." She squeezed my arm. "Let's go get 'em."

Loud, angry barks, high-pitched yapping, whining, crying, and howling hit me from all sides. There were kennels that housed as many as six little ones and others that had signs that said MUST BE ALONE. I stood frozen for a second and took in the rows and rows of cages.

Big sad eyes looked back at me from the closest kennels, noses pressed through the bars for a soft rub, and desperate paws tried to touch my legs, my arms, and my face as I knelt down beside their cages.

Tongues tried to lick my cheeks, my fingers; anything to be seen and noticed. "Take me! Take me!" they all seemed to say in their whining and whimpering and barking voices. As I moved down the rows, there were some that jumped and barked, baring their teeth, and others that stood huddled like frightened deer in the backs of the cages. But most of them came right up to the gates in the kennels, wanting every part of me. There were purebreds and mutts all mingled together; shepherds and pit bulls and schnauzers and poodles. There were huskies and Chihuahuas and mastiffs and mountain dogs. There were some that had some of this and some of that all thrown together to make an adorable mutt. Some were fat while others were thin and mangy. It seemed that there were no two alike. But what they all shared in common was that they no longer belonged. Anywhere or to anyone. Discarded dogs and some that jumped fences and walked through open gates and went missing, like Danny.

I made it through that first day at the shelter by staying focused and giving as much love as I could to as many dogs as I could. I held the little ones close and gently stroked the big ones and gave them belly rubs. I fed them, cleaned their kennels, and had to laugh once when I thought about what Kate must be doing right now on a Saturday afternoon: probably lying with a mud pack on her face in a spa while I was covered with it and worse!

At the end of the afternoon, while we washed up and got ready to leave, I told Rayleen of my fears that Danny was in a shelter somewhere far away. He had been gone for five days and today would be the day they could put him down!

"I've checked most of 'em in California for you already, but let's do it again just to be sure."

We went online and scoured the pictures of every border collie in shelters from here to Sacramento, but none of them was Danny.

While we were looking, Lulu sent me a text message asking if I wanted to sleep over tonight, but I knew all I'd want to do when I got home was take a shower and go to bed early. Officer Reyes kept looking over at me, so Rayleen introduced me to him.

"You're right by the ocean. That's a nice place to live," Officer Reyes said when Rayleen introduced me as "Bree from Santa Monica."

"Yes, it is," I replied, and noticed how lined his face looked.

"When I retire next year, that's what I'll do. I'll go to the beach and listen to the sound of the waves. It will be good to get away from the barking." He looked at me with eyes that were gray and flat.

As Rayleen and I made our way down the corridor, I thought how sad it was that Officer Reyes seemed to have lost interest in caring for the animals around him. They all seemed to blur one into another for him now.

The New Hope coordinator was a young African American man named Steve Samuels, whose main job it was to get the word out to rescue organizations to save the "last call" dogs, as he referred to them.

"I want to help the dogs get homes," I told him and Rayleen.

"Hey, we need some young enthusiasm around here," Steve said, patting my shoulder. "I'm serious. I send out the same old emails to the same rescue people in big red letters with pleas to save these dogs from death row, but it seems like everyone is overloaded. You come up with a new idea to get them out and I'm all ears, Bree."

Steve thanked Rayleen for bringing me and she seemed pleased that I had turned out to be such a trouper.

"That's my gal." She gave me a big hug. "Told ya you could do it!"

As we drove back to Santa Monica on the freeway I felt something inside me lift, like a giant weight. I had done something meaningful and important today and it wasn't for myself. New Hope Steve and Rayleen had really appreciated what I had done at the shelter today. I really liked how it made me feel.

Chapter Twelve

"Daddy!" His spicy aftershave wafted over me as I opened the front door.

He stood in the entrance hall in his khaki slacks and blue blazer with his arms stretched out wide. I dropped my purse and ran into them.

"You smell so good!" I breathed against his white Oxford shirt.

"Can't say the same about you!" He chuckled, but pulled me in even closer. "Smells like you've been cleaning Soprano's stable with Lulu."

"No! Not horses. Dogs."

At the word "dog," he released me and looked into

my eyes. "I can't believe he's not here." He ran a big hand through his thatch of hair. "The house feels ridiculously empty. . . ."

"I know," I said softly. "I can't believe Mom let him get out."

"Look, you have every right to be upset, but it was a mistake, Bree."

I wasn't up for a long discussion about my mom right now.

"Can we talk about this later, Dad? I gotta take a shower."

"Sure, kiddo. I'll be in the bedroom unpacking.

I lay on my bed and closed my eyes. The sound of dogs barking and whimpering filled every inch of my head. My ears rang with their cries. The shelter had followed me home. Not just in the grime under my nails or the stains on my jeans or the animal scent that clung to me. The shelter dogs had gotten under my skin, crawled their way into my veins, jumped inside my limbs, burrowed into my muscles. They curled up behind my closed eyelids. I felt the pain of all the abandoned dogs at the shelter who might never make it out alive. I must have fallen into a long, deep sleep because when I woke up my room was mottled in purple shadow.

As I sat up a strange, excited feeling washed over me.

I knew what I had to do. I needed to save as many of

the shelters dogs as I could. I, Bree Davies, could make a difference in their lives. All I had to do was figure out how. I was so lost in thought that I was startled when my cell phone rang.

"Hey, Bree."

I paused before realizing who it was.

"Ashton," I said, sitting up with a jolt.

"Yeah, you okay? You sound kinda confused."

"I've never been clearer." I felt the blood rush to my head.

"So, tomorrow. We still on?" I could hear the electronic collisions of video games in the background.

"Yeah. That would be great." I wanted to tell Ashton about all the dogs I'd met downtown but decided it would be better in person.

"Cool. I'll see you at, like, noon?"

"Sure. That's fine. You've got my address?"

"It's in the school directory, right?" I heard a loud crash and guessed he must have wiped out in his game.

After we hung up I made a "To Do" list.

1. Find Danny: Ashton/more flyers, internet, door to door.
2. Talk to Rayleen and Steve/New Hope

coordinator on Monday or sooner about how I can help the shelter dogs.
3. Get Lulu and others from school involved once I get the okay from above.
4. Try very hard to get back to getting As.
5. Stop by and say hi to Martha and help in garden, if needed.
6. Pray every night that Danny is safe.

The one thing that wasn't on the list was what to do about me and my mom, since I really didn't have a clue how even to begin fixing things between us.

Epiphany: a sudden, intuitive perception or insight into the reality or essential meaning of something, usually initiated by some experience.

I text messaged Lulu and told her that there was something really important I wanted to talk to her about and she should call me immediately. But she wrote back and said, *Riding Soprano now—don't worry, I'm being careful. Then violin lesson, will call after xoxo.*

Just a few days ago the first thing I would've wanted her to know was that Ashton was coming over, and while I was glad that he was going to hang out with me, what I really wanted to talk to her about was the shelter and figuring out a way to save the dogs.

Chapter Thirteen

While I sat next to my dad at the sushi bar, he mixed the wasabi and soy sauce into a paste with one chopstick like he always did. As a welcome-home treat he took me to dinner at my favorite sushi restaurant. He knew I loved the spicy tuna hand rolls that Nayago, the owner and chef, had been making for me since I was about seven. I was all cleaned and showered and felt truly hungry for the first time in days. The newsmom was working late at the station so it was just the two of us.

Nayago's restaurant was on the corner of San Vicente Boulevard and Twenty-fourth Street. It was surrounded by a trendy coffee house, a hair salon, and a yoga studio, so the people coming in were either carrying yoga mats and had wet, stringy hair, or were perfectly groomed and reeked of hair mousse and lattes. Nayago's also attracted all the Brentwood and Santa Monica locals, some of whom were pretty famous, but the number one rule if you lived among celebrities and stars was to ignore them and let them eat their sushi in peace.

I smiled at Nayago, with his brown, twinkly eyes and bright red kimono jacket, as he set my plate down in front of me. He always told me that I was his favorite twelve-year-old, ten-year-old, or eight-year-old, depending on what age I was at the time.

"Bree," my dad said as he chewed on an edamame bean. "I know your mom's career has a lot to do with why you feel so let down by her."

"She's never around, Dad."

"I know." He took a long sip of green tea.

"And she lost Danny."

"It was an accident."

"Right, but that doesn't change the fact that he's gone." I dipped my spoon into the hot miso soup.

"Being a news anchor is something your mom's wanted since I met her when she was a communications major in college. She's never been closer to getting an anchor position than she is now."

"That's great, Dad. Then I guess I'll be seeing her even less."

Nayago handed me the spicy tuna hand roll.

"No, the whole thing with Danny has her really upset. She's thinking of cutting back her hours at the station, actually."

"Then she'll never be an anchor."

"That's right," my dad said slowly and deliberately. "Sometimes you have to make decisions like that."

"I don't want her quitting because of Danny." I wiped my hands on a napkin. "And I don't want her staying home just because she feels guilty."

After dinner my dad suggested that we take a walk, so after thanking Nayago, we headed out of the restaurant in the direction of the ocean.

San Vicente Boulevard is known for its long center isle of beautiful coral trees and green grass, which is the perfect stretch for joggers, cyclists, and walkers to get some decent exercise. Most people started at the end of Brentwood where the boulevard began and ran, biked, or walked all the way down to Ocean Avenue, which was my favorite street. It sat on a bluff high above the sparkling Pacific Ocean below. It was well worth the sweat and pain to reach the end of a run and look down at the sandy white beach and expanse of blue ocean. I would walk Danny to Ocean Avenue, which wasn't far from our house, at around sunset at least three times a week.

The sun looked like spilled orange juice across the sky, and if I was lucky enough to catch it as it went down, I'd always make a wish. Different ones at different times. One of my wishes was that Danny and I would be together always. "Make a wish Danny-O. Look at the sunset," I would say, and rub my hand in his soft fur. He'd look up at me confused about what I meant. "Okay, then, I'll have to make one for you." I would try and imagine what a dog would wish for. A big juicy bone? A playdate with the pretty golden retriever down the road? A long sleep in a big comfy bed?

As I walked with my dad toward the bluff, I thought of how different my doggy wishes would be for Danny now. To never get lost, or be put into a shelter. Or worse, euthanized.

"So, who's this hippie woman Mom says took you to the shelter?" my dad asked as we picked up our pace.

"Hippie! Is that what mom called Rayleen?" I had to laugh.

"'Bohemian,' was actually what she said."

"What does that mean?"

"Someone unconventional, a free spirit."

"That's hilarious, Dad. Just because she happens to wear cargo pants and flip-flops and not heels and Chanel suits that makes her a bohemian hippie?" I skirted around two women who were walking at a leisurely pace. "She's awesome and she saves dog's lives. I want you to meet her. You'll like her."

"Sure," my dad said. "Let me know when."

"How about now?"

My dad looked down at his watch.

"Okay. We have time. It's early enough," he said in his warm, agreeable way.

I stopped and leaned against one of the giant coral trees, its large trunk the perfect place to rest my head. I was puffing and panting just a little. Walking fast after eating was never ideal. I reached for my cell phone in my back pocket and scrolled through my address book until I found Rayleen's number. It rang four or five times. I was about to hang up when she answered.

"Rayleen, it's me, Bree."

"I know that, sweet pea, your name came up on the ID thingy."

"Can I come over?" I asked, then added quickly, "My dad's in town and he really wants to meet you."

I could hear barking in the background.

"Sure. Just me and the dogs kicking back on a Saturday night, howlin' at the full moon."

I laughed, mostly because it was dusk and not quite night yet, and there certainly wasn't a full moon out yet.

"She said yes." I handed my dad the phone so Rayleen could give him directions to her house.

Chapter Fourteen

On the way up Topanga Canyon's mountainous road of twists and turns and long stretches where the world outside was empty and black, my dad and I talked about Danny for a long time. He told me how guilty he felt because he wasn't in town when Danny ran off. I told him that I felt like a piece of me was missing, but then told him about the shelter and why it was so important.

I could see his smile in the dark, his straight, white teeth flashing. "I'm proud of you, kiddo." He reached over and squeezed my hand across the seat.

"Don't be proud till I've done something, Dad."

* * *

It took us an extra fifteen minutes to actually find Rayleen's house. She was right, it was buried way, way up the canyon on a dirt road that led to nothing but shrubbery and trees.

We almost had to feel our way through all the overgrown bush in the dark to find the entrance, but eventually we found the front door and I lifted the oversized knocker, which was in the shape of a tortoise.

It was hard to introduce my dad to Rayleen over the dogs trying to greet us at the door. They were a pack, that's for sure, and they all jumped and barked as Rayleen tried to quiet them.

"Allakazam!" she yelled, and amazingly they all stopped and went to lie in their doggy beds, which were scattered around the room. "My grandpa the magician taught me that trick." She winked. "Works like a charm."

Rayleen's house was something like I had imagined, only better. On every surface there were gold-colored candles of every shape and size, and sweet-spicy incense was burning. There were no chairs to sit on, only giant-sized velvet cushions that were scattered among the doggy beds.

"Keeps us all on the same level." She curled up on a large, red velvet cushion and patted for me to sit down on the green one next to her. My dad stood uncomfortably shifting from one leg to the other.

"I am so sorry, Mr. Davies, for the lack of appropriate chairs, but there's a chest if you'd like to sit on it." Her southern drawl came out slow and sugary. She pointed to a mahogany chest and my dad coughed and sat and stretched his long legs out in front of him. One of the dogs got off his mat and went over to sniff him. He looked like a giant, black, shaggy terrier.

"Well, what do we have here, a scruffy muppet monster?" My dad patted the dog on the head.

Rayleen laughed. She was wearing low-slung jeans and a belt with a big rodeo buckle. She had on cowboy boots and a checkered shirt. I knew the newsdad, being a reporter, had already made a mental note of everything about her and every detail in the room. I imagined him sharing his impression of Rayleen with my mom later. "Well, she's more like a New Age cowgirl who herds dogs instead of cattle."

Rayleen offered us mint tea and agave, a natural cactus sweetener that looked like honey but tasted better. She told us the names of each of the rescue dogs. There were ten, including Clay, who came right over to me and licked my hand softly. He lay down next to me as I sipped the sweet tea, and I rubbed his back.

"Alfie's the big muppet monster," she told us. "Found

him half dead in the middle of the road in Alabama, but now look at him." She pointed at Alfie, who now had his shaggy head resting on my dad's lap. "Fat 'n' sassy. That's what five years of good livin' will do for a dog."

She went around the room and pointed to each one and introduced them to us like you would a friend. There was Mr. P, a four-pound Chihuahua who bit everyone, including Rayleen; there was Raka, a German shepherd who she got for twenty dollars from a homeless man who had been beating her; and Woof the wolfhound, who came from a sanctuary that was forced to close because of lack of money; there was Matteo, a bug-eyed white Pekingese pulled from a shelter in the nick of time; and Matilda, a beagle who was abandoned in the yard of a home when the owners moved away. There were three strays Rayleen had found hungry and starving and skinny on the streets of downtown LA not too long ago. Their names were Belinda, Chadney, and Maddy, all sweet mutts who were a mix of this and that. Rayleen was fattening them up before she found them homes.

The newsdad seemed impressed. "You do good work."

"It's not my work. It's my calling."

"Like she has to do it, Dad," I said.

Rayleen had explained to me in the car coming home from the shelter that animal rescue was something she felt chosen to do by a force greater than herself. A higher power, she called it. I wondered if only special people got to be chosen to have a calling.

"I know what a calling is, Bree," my dad said quietly.

"Do you have a calling, Dad?" I asked and put my head down on Clay's neck.

He cleared his throat. The candlelight flickered and I felt like everything around us had gotten spooky quiet. Even the dogs were still, all sprawled out and sleeping.

"Well, that's an interesting question. No one's ever asked me that." His eyes seemed to mist over and he shifted his square jaw from side to side. "I think I hoped to enlighten people with what I had to say in my reporting. But I guess I spend most of my time writing nasty details about nasty situations."

Rayleen lit another stick of incense, and her green eyes looked sparkly bright just before the match went out.

"I feel there's a book in you, Mr. Davies. Then you can say all you really want."

My dad rubbed his chin. "Funny, I've always wanted to write about my experiences and observations around the world. I've never told anyone about it before."

"It was just a hunch." Rayleen turned and smiled sweetly and asked my dad if it would be okay to leave me with her for a while. The newsdad made a quick phone call to a photographer friend who also lived up in Topanga Canyon. He was home and my dad said he'd go there for an hour or so and then be back to get me.

"Sounds grand to me." Rayleen stretched her hands above her head and arched her back like a cat.

I knew my dad was being extra nice to me tonight by agreeing to leave me alone with Rayleen. I felt like he was making more effort with me during this hard time.

Rayleen took the teacup from my dad's hand and he looked at her earnestly.

"You'll help us find Danny, won't you?"

"Yes, sir. Already am. I can't wait to meet him."

"You think he'll come back?"

Rayleen paused for a moment and sucked in air. "He'll be back. When the time's right."

She walked my dad to the door and shook his hand in a very formal way. "It was a pleasure meeting you, Mr. Davies. I'll keep your lovely gal safe an' warm till you come back."

Rayleen put on some strange music and I asked her what it was.

"Monks chanting in a monastery in Tibet, sweet pea. The sound's good for healing the soul, humans and animals both. I play it every night for the pack. It's like their bedtime lullaby."

My dad left me at Rayleen's house for only two hours, but it felt like he was gone for days. Rayleen and I talked and talked, back and forth with such ease, like a river that flowed downward and deeper, while the dogs stirred and slept. It seemed like time had slunk away. It wasn't important or wanted here. There was nothing pushing Rayleen to be somewhere else or hurrying her in any way. She focused all her attention on me as we sat cross-legged facing each other on the cushions.

"I grew up on a farm just outside of Savannah, Georgia. Lotsa goats an' chickens an' horses as well as dogs an' cats roamin' around. I loved it there." She sighed. "But then when I was ten, everythin' changed. Papa lost the farm and we moved to New Orleans. The only thing he did all day was play cards an' smoke three packs of cigarettes."

"How did you get money for food and clothes?" I asked.

"Mama cleaned rich people's houses for a while, but then a massive heart attack killed Papa and Mama used the life insurance money to open the kinda store she'd always wanted."

Rayleen told me about her mother's homeopathic

cures and the herb shop she opened on Bourbon Street. They lived above it, and in the morning Rayleen would have to step over men who had passed out on the sidewalk from drinking all night so she could get to the bus to school.

"Wow. That sounds so different," I said.

"Oh, it certainly was that. I discovered my everlastin' need to rescue animals around then. I took in the stray, skinny cats and an occasional dog from the streets. My mama didn't mind much. She was always mixing something and giving a cure to someone. Busy, busy always an' not mindin' me much."

"Sounds like my mom." I stretched out long on the floor and looked up at the ceiling. It was painted deep turquoise, the color of a Caribbean sea.

"She's doing the best that she knows how, sweet pea. And she loves you. You need to know that."

"She loves her career more."

Rayleen was quiet for a minute and then spoke.

"I have a feeling lots is about to change with your mama."

The candles flickered and the monks chanted.

"That would be nice." I sighed.

That night Rayleen and I talked about a hundred different things while the candles burned lower and lower and the incense dissolved into ashes.

"What's school like?" she asked.

"Good mostly, but one of my best friends and I are kinda drifting apart."

Rayleen stroked the top of Alfie's head. He had fallen asleep beside her.

"That happens, sweet pea. Sometimes we just need a break from someone, and then when we get back together, it's all good as new again."

"Well, I've made a new friend, a boy."

She took a long sip of tea and smiled. "What's his name?"

I told her all about Ashton and his soon-to-be wicked stepmother. Rayleen predicted that Stephanie wouldn't be in his life much longer and that Ashton didn't need to worry about Buster and Bullwinkle.

"He loves dogs, too," I said.

"I like him already," Rayleen said. "Bring him to the shelter sometime."

"I will."

It was so easy to talk to Rayleen. Thoughts and feelings and words poured out of me like the sweet agave she had stirred into my tea. Just as I heard my dad's Range Rover come to a crunching stop outside, I told Rayleen that I really wanted to help the shelter dogs.

"I want to figure out a way to get them out of the shelter and into homes where they can sleep on warm doggy beds and get kisses and hugs and lots of walks and food every day from owners who will love them for the rest of their lives."

Rayleen sat still and quiet and closed her eyes. "You'll find a way." A smile formed on her lips. "I know you will."

She opened her eyes and stood up and came over to my cushion and held my hand in hers.

"Synchronicity, sweet pea. Synchronicity." She leaned forward and kissed me lightly on the forehead just as my dad knocked on the front door.

Later that night when I got home I looked up the word "synchronicity," since it had never been a vocab word and I didn't have a clue what it meant.

Synchronicity: the coincidental occurrence of events and especially psychic events (as similar thoughts in widely separated persons or a mental image of an unexpected event before it happens) that seem related but are not explained by conventional mechanisms of causality.

Chapter Fifteen

"She sounds weird," Ashton said as we walked door to door dropping off flyers that read LOST DOG! REWARD!!

"She's different. Not weird. And you should like her already since she thinks your dad's fiancée will be out of your life soon."

"Yeah, right." Ashton threw a baseball up in the air and caught it in his mitt. He had come straight from practice and was still in his uniform. "She's got a contractor and the architect over today. Wants to tear down and change everything in the house. Ugh! I just wish my dad was in town."

"Where is he?" I asked.

"Shooting a movie. Where else?"

"Cool."

"Not really. He's gone all the time directing the sequel of the sequel of whatever."

"My mom's gone a ton, too, and my dad even more. I wish they had normal jobs sometimes."

"Like what?" Ashton asked.

"A doctor, an accountant, a hairdresser, I dunno. Just something that lets them come home every day at normal hours."

"At least your mom comes home at all. Mine's MIA."

"I'm sorry," I said, and really meant it.

I was trying hard to keep up with Ashton. I was wearing a dress, something I didn't often do, and now I wished I was in more comfortable leggings instead. My feet were still blistered, so going door to door was painful but necessary.

My mother had raised an eyebrow when I'd come down for breakfast earlier. She and my dad were sipping coffee and eating low carb, no trans fat muffins under the shaded cabana by the pool.

"What's the occasion?" she had asked.

My dad had *The Washington Post* up over his

face but lowered it. He looked me up and down and smiled.

"Very beautiful. My little girl's all grown up." He patted for me to sit beside him.

"Ashton Adams is coming over." I tried to sound as "no-big-deal" casual as possible.

"Another rehearsal?" my mom asked.

"No. He's helping me find Danny."

"That's very nice of him." My mother winked at my dad. They gave each other stupid, wiggly smiles that were hard to miss.

"Stop! He loves dogs, too, that's all." I didn't need to be teased about anything this morning. I was nervous enough as it was.

After that, the newsparents dropped the whole Ashton subject and we had a reasonably pleasant breakfast together, except for the giant glaring hole under the center of the table—a black and white dog who would normally be begging for scraps at our feet.

When we were just about out of flyers, I asked Ashton if he'd mind if we stopped off at one more house that was just a few blocks over. I had been getting these weird feelings in my gut about Martha, the old woman who had found Danny's collar, and I wanted to make sure she was okay. We walked over to Marguerita Avenue to

Martha's white-shuttered house.

The first thing I noticed as we went up her driveway was that the rows of yellow daffodils that led up to her front door were wilted and dying, and the front garden looked like it hadn't been watered in a while. I knocked on the door, but there was no answer so I knocked again. Still nothing.

"The ol' lady's not here. Let's go." Ashton turned and started heading down the driveway, tossing his baseball in the air as he walked.

I got this weird, fluttery tightness in my stomach. I knew I couldn't leave. I tried the door handle and it opened with ease.

"I got in. Come back!" I shouted.

"C'mon, Bree, we're wasting time. I still wanna go online and post Danny's picture on Craigslist."

But I knew something was wrong. I stepped over the threshold into Martha's house.

The first thing that struck me was how dark it was inside. All the shades were drawn and there was a damp, moldy smell in the house. I remembered how sparkly clean and neat everything had been the last time I was here, but now the place was a mess.

"Martha," I called. "Martha, it's me, Bree, the girl with the lost dog."

A strange croaking noise came out of a bedroom. I

walked quickly to the door and opened it. Martha lay, small and deathly white, in her bed. She tried to raise a withered hand, but it fell helplessly back to her side.

"Martha! What happened to you!" I went quickly to her just as I heard Ashton yell from the other room.

"Oh my God! This place reeks!"

Martha's eyes were hollow and scared looking, like a small animal caught in a trap. She tried to speak, but her mouth was dry and cracked at the corners.

"Call nine one one!" I shouted to Ashton.

I took Martha's hand in mine. "It's okay. You're not alone anymore. Help is on its way." Words came out of me that I'd only seen on a TV medical crisis show. She curled her frail fingers around mine like a claw and held on tight. A parched cry came out of her. I could see the tears without liquid form in her eyes. She was beyond dehydrated, just like her garden.

Ashton stood in the doorway of Martha's bedroom. He spoke quickly to the 911 operator on his cell phone.

"She's very old and looks very bad. We found her . . . yes. What's the address, Bree?" I didn't know the house number, so he ran outside to get it.

In less than two minutes we heard the sirens blaring. The Santa Monica Fire Department and an ambulance arrived and they instantly went into high gear. I stayed with Martha the whole time, while Ashton answered their questions. "Is she her granddaughter?" I heard one paramedic ask as they watched the way Martha clung to me.

"No, just a neighbor," Ashton told them.

I watched as the team put an oxygen mask on Martha and took her blood pressure and started IV fluids through one of the small purple veins in her arm, and thought how strange it was that in just a week I had been called someone's daughter and granddaughter when neither was true. Still, Rayleen and Martha somehow felt like family to me.

They wheeled Martha out of her house on a gurney.

"Can I go with her in the ambulance?" I asked one of the paramedics, but he said it wasn't possible since I was under age and there was no adult other than Martha present.

"I'll be by to see you as soon as you come home. Promise," I told her as her fluttering, paper-thin eyelids closed and they hoisted her into the ambulance.

As they got ready to leave, the same paramedic turned to us and said that Martha had probably been alone in the house for days and had definitely not eaten or had anything to drink for more than forty-eight hours.

"If you hadn't come over to her house, she might not have made it through the night. You did a good deed, young lady, young man." The firefighter patted my shoulder and shook Ashton's hand, which he took out of his glove.

"How'd you know something was wrong?" Ashton asked as we walked back to my house.

"Just a hunch," I said. It was the same thing Rayleen had said about my dad's book. "Just a hunch."

We were both quiet for a while. The incident with Martha had really shaken me up, and I guessed it had affected Ashton, too. I started thinking about how lonely Martha was now that her husband was gone and how nice it would be for her to have a companion, a friend, someone who cared about her and that she could care about. She needed company, someone to snuggle on the couch and watch TV with and to talk to while she ate dinner.

Thoughts of Danny suddenly flashed through my brain. Love, comfort, friendship, and belonging. Images of the shelter dogs, sad and unloved, followed.

I grabbed Ashton's arm. "I've got it!" I said excitedly.

"Got what?" Ashton looked at me confused.

"A dog! That's what Martha needs. A shelter dog!"

"A what?" Ashton and I stood at the gates of my house. I pulled him down to sit in the same spot on the curb where I had waited for Danny to come back. I needed to explain everything to him. The shelter and all the abandoned animals that might get euthanized any day. The words tumbled out of me so fast, in one long, disjointed sentence that never seemed to end, but Ashton kept his eyes intently focused on me the whole time.

"Martha," I said, finally catching my breath, "should adopt a shelter dog."

"What about all the rest that are left?" Ashton said with a serious look on his face.

"I know. And there are so many."

"There's got to be a way to save them," Ashton said.

"It's about finding people who could really benefit from having a dog in their lives. Maybe they don't even realize it. . . ."

"And maybe they just don't know how many dogs really need homes," Ashton added.

"Well, if I can try to match Martha with a dog, why can't I match other people with other dogs?"

"Sure, why not?" Ashton grinned.

"I'm going to ask Rayleen and Steve if I can put on an adoption day at the shelter and invite everyone I know—"

"And people you don't know," Ashton said excitedly. "Advertise the event online: emails, websites, blogs, whatever you can to get them to come."

"Dogs for people and people for dogs." I stood up

and smiled. "Rayleen said I'd figure out a way. And I have!"

"Now you've just got to get the shelter guy to agree to let you do it," Ashton said as we walked up the front steps.

Ashton stayed over until almost dinnertime. We took my laptop down to the living room and Ashton took charge and posted pictures of Danny and information about him on websites that dealt with everything from lost dogs to lost shoelaces. When he was done, we talked nonstop about how to make the adoption day a big success. Ashton was really excited about it and said to count him in. I wasn't surprised. Dog lovers stuck together, didn't they?

When his driver picked him up, I waved good-bye and I felt a fuzzy, warm feeling inside as they drove away. Ashton wasn't anything like I thought he was, now that I was getting to know him better. My dad always said you should never take things at face value and you always have to dig deep to find out what the real story is and what is the truth.

I called Lulu and I filled her in on all the events of the day.

"I can't believe Ashton just left. Wow!" she said.

"He's helping me find Danny."

Lulu let out one of her famous loud whistles. I had to laugh.

She promised she'd come and help me put up flyers and canvass the neighborhood the next day. I knew she had a million extracurricular activities, so I really appreciated her wanting to help.

"That's what best friends are for, right?" she said.

I told her all about the adoption day idea that I still hadn't discussed with Rayleen or New Hope Steve.

"If it happens, I'm there with whipped cream and a cherry on top."

"How about dog bones instead of cherries?" I said.

"Even better," Lulu replied.

Chapter Sixteen

Over the next few days we got about twenty emails and calls from people who thought they had found Danny, some as far away as Bakersfield and San Diego. But after talking to each of them, it turned out they weren't Danny, but other lost dogs. I took down their numbers and gave them to Rayleen, who was now up to fifteen dogs at her house. She was up and down the freeway every day, picking up the "Danny dogs" from all over. Some near, some far.

"Your Danny boy is doing good work, even though he's not around. He's savin' other dogs who are lost, stray, or dumped!" I knew Rayleen would find them all homes if she couldn't find their owners, and that none of the new rescues would land at the shelter. But with every call or email my hopes soared, then plummeted. I asked the people who contacted me to email pictures of the dog they had found. My heart raced every time I went to my in-box, sure that this would be the one. Then I'd click on the attachment only to see the face of a dog that was adorable but not mine.

The longer Danny was gone, the greater my fear became that I would never find him.

"Have faith, sweet pea. What does your heart tell you, not your frightened brain?" Rayleen said as we drove to the shelter after school so I could talk to Steve, the New Hope coordinator.

I closed my eyes and tried to make my brain stop for a second. I pictured Danny, then felt him in my heart. Only then did Danny become a beat inside me, clear and strong. I opened my eyes.

"He's alive," I said softly to Rayleen.

"See, that's called trustin' your intuition not your mind." She tapped the side of her head. "Thoughts can be big troublemakers." She laughed. "Listen to Elvis the King. 'We can't go on together with suspicious minds,' she sang along with her car stereo.

* * *

While I was at the shelter, I saw Officer Reyes sitting at his desk eating his lunch alone. When I made my way toward him, he smiled and seemed genuinely pleased to see me.

"Care for a bean burrito?" he asked.

"No, but thanks anyway." There was something I wanted to ask him that I had been thinking about since I first saw how he was when Neptune came in.

I cleared my throat. "Officer Reyes, I hope you don't mind my asking, but after a while, are the dogs and cats that come in here just a blur to you?"

Officer Reyes looked at me and nodded. "I'm afraid so, young lady."

"I understand," I said, then proceeded to tell him all about my adoption day idea.

"I am happy to hear it. I hope you get the okay to do it," he said.

"Can I make a deal with you?" I said.

"What's that?" He shuffled through some papers on his overcrowded desk.

"If I get all the red listed dogs saved at my adoption day, will you try to start looking at the animals again as they come in?"

He paused and held my gaze. "You are a sassy but very smart young lady," he said. "Okay, deal." He held his rough, calloused hand out toward me. We shook.

Now I really had to make sure that I got the approval for the event, since getting Officer Reyes to care about the animals again and not treat them like inventory would be really great.

I checked on Neptune. He was in a cage with three other big dogs, and much to my relief wasn't red listed yet. He ate the dog biscuit that I gave him, then slunk to the back of the kennel with his tail between his legs. He lay down and closed his eyes, and I imagined that he was wishing this was all a bad dream and that the next time he woke up he'd be outside rolling on cool grass, not lying, fighting for space, on cold concrete.

As I turned away from Neptune's cage, it suddenly hit me. Martha would be the one to give Neptune a loving home! He would give her a reason to get up in the morning. She'd have to feed him and walk him, and he'd keep her company while she gardened. She had called yesterday when I got home from school to let me know she was out of the hospital. "Home and alive, apparently thanks to you." Her voice was crackly and weak.

I had finished my homework as quickly as I could and had raced over to her house. Martha had told me how being alone day after day had finally gotten to her and so she had climbed into bed and just didn't get out, until Ashton and I showed up.

"There was no one around to cook for or pick up

after. Everything felt pointless." She coughed. "I'm used to caring for others. I like being needed. It gives me a purpose."

"Call me if you feel sad and lonely," I told her.

She said she would.

I could barely feel my feet touch the ground as I ran through the shelter to find Rayleen. She was with Steve in his office. I told them all about Martha and how bad she'd felt since her husband had died and how a dog would be exactly what she needed and that Neptune was just the perfect one for her. I talked so fast I'm sure they only understood every third word I said, but Rayleen got the picture.

"Well, that's a grand idea, sweet pea, but shouldn't we check with ol' Martha first? She might not even like dogs."

"She'll love him! I know she will," I said excitedly.

Steve smiled. "That enthusiasm needs to be bottled and distributed around here."

"Well"—I took a deep breath—"I have a very enthusiastic idea for you both." I looked from Steve to Rayleen. "I want to put on an adoption day at the shelter and invite tons of people and get all the red listed dogs adopted before they're put to sleep."

Steve looked from me to Rayleen and back again.

Rayleen nodded and smiled. "That's the best idea I've heard since coming to California." She turned to Steve. "Sounds like a win-win to me."

"Hmm." He scratched his chin. "It's an excellent thought, Bree." Steve rapped his knuckles on his desk. "Gotta work out all the details, but like I always say to my staff, a fresh and eager volunteer with great ideas is never someone to be ignored." He looked over at me. "Do you think you can spread the word fast?"

I nodded, unable to speak.

"It has to be this Saturday if you want to save the current red listed dogs. This weekend is all the time most of them have left."

"So that's a yes?" Rayleen said slowly.

"It's a yes." Steve grinned.

I ran around his desk and gave him a big hug.

"'Save a shelter dog. Mutts are miracles.' That's what I want the banner outside to say," I blurted out.

"She's the greatest." Steve looked at Rayleen.

"Told ya." Rayleen smiled back.

Rayleen convinced Steve to put an "interested party" notation in Neptune's file. That would buy a little time for me to talk to Martha and guarantee that Neptune wouldn't be red listed yet, but time was of the essence to get him out.

Chapter Seventeen

I was in a good mood when I walked into the house, and was surprised to see the newsmom, who wasn't due back until the evening, in the living room pacing.

"I've been home for an hour. I thought you'd have been back long ago."

"You knew I was with Rayleen at the shelter." I pointed to my jeans, which were covered in filth from cleaning out the kennels.

"Oh, I planned to get home early so we could go to the mall or catch a movie," she said brightly. "A fun mother-daughter afternoon. What do you think? It's still early enough."

"I'm really tired, Mom," I said quietly. "Thanks, but not today."

"Well, that's a shame. I had hoped we could spend some quality time together." She pursed her lips. "You've still got to go out and have some fun, honey. The shelter's a depressing place, isn't it?"

"No. It's an important place," I said, then added, "and I'm needed and wanted there."

"You're needed and wanted here," she said.

"That's news to me," I said.

"Don't start up, Bree, I was trying to do something nice. . . ."

"You don't get it, do you?" I held her gaze. "You think one afternoon is going to do it? You're never around long enough to really know me."

"I see that, honey." She walked toward me. "I want to make things right between us." She reached to touch my arm, but I pulled it back.

"It'll take more than a mall and movie afternoon, Mom."

We stood facing each other.

"The truth is I feel closer to Rayleen than I do to you. She'd make a better mom."

I watched as her hand flew to cover her mouth.

I knew I had gone too far and wished I could take

the words back right as I spoke them, but they hit her like a barrage of arrows. I watched her face go ashen white and her lips start to tremble. She took a step back away from me, like I was a criminal.

"I came home early to tell you that I'm cutting back on my hours at the station so I can be home more." Her voice quivered. "But I guess it really doesn't matter now, does it?" She turned and walked unsteadily on her high heels from the room.

"Mom!" I yelled after her. "I didn't mean it!" But she slammed the living room door shut behind her.

The newsmom closed herself in her office and I spent the afternoon in my bedroom.

I sat and stared at myself in my mirror. My mom and I had the same nose, the same chin, even the same arch in our eyebrows. I wondered how two people who looked so alike could be so different and not get along? I had been angry about her TV career since I was a little girl because it took her away from me. Now she was ready to stay home more. But somehow, I couldn't accept it. Why was she making this decision now? Was it all because of Danny? I wanted her to explain to me why, but she was really hurt and mad right now.

I had so many questions swirling around my head, and I still needed to put together the email that I was going to send out for the adoption day on Saturday. Steve had given me a list of people who had donated time or money or expressed interest in helping the shelter, and I was going to spread the word through his email list as well as my own. I also had a whole scene to memorize from *A Midsummer Night's Dream*, since Ashton and I had our final rehearsal tomorrow before we had to perform for our drama class on Friday afternoon. I felt sick to my stomach about everything. My cell phone rang and I was relieved to have a distraction from my growing anxiety. It was a very stuff-sounding Lulu.

"You sound awful!" I said.

"Got a really bad cold." She blew her nose, loudly.

"Guess you're not up to posting flyers?"

"Sorry, too sick to walk around, but at least your boyfriend, Ashton, helped put up some." She coughed.

"He is not my boyfriend, okay? He's a boy who's a friend."

"Everyone's saying so."

"Everyone is wrong."

"Okay, okay. I didn't call to argue. What can I do to help while I'm lying sick in bed?" she asked.

"Call all the vets on the west side to see if Danny's maybe there. I've done it three times already. You can take over that job. I'll send you the list."

"Done." Lulu blew her nose.

"Thanks, Lulu. Do you think you'll be well enough to come help with my adoption event downtown on Saturday?"

"You got the approval?" she said, sounding as excited as she could while running a fever and coughing.

"Yes! This Saturday afternoon."

"Awesome! Only one small problem. Kate's birthday party is the same afternoon."

"Oh, no. I totally forgot," I said.

"How are we both going to tell her we can't make it? She'll be crushed," Lulu said.

"You have to go," I said softly. I really wanted Lulu with me at the adoption event, but we couldn't both let Kate down.

"We'll figure it out," Lulu said, then sneezed. "Look, things change. You didn't expect to be looking for your lost dog and putting on an adoption event. Right?"

"That's true," I said slowly. "Things really do change quickly."

When we hung up the phone, I remembered something I had read in a bathroom stall at the mall a few months back. It stood out among the scribbles that said things like "Tiffany was here 2/11/09" or "My boyfriend rocks!" It was written in a very bold, black marker so it was hard to miss. It said, "The only thing in life that's constant is change." As Lulu, Kate, and I went from store to store, trying on clothes and jewelry and stopping to eat frozen yogurt in the food court, I couldn't get the words out of my mind.

Lying on my bed now, they came back to me and made perfect sense. The only thing in life that's constant is change.

My life had to shift drastically in order for me to get the meaning.

Only now did I understand. Good or bad, nothing stayed the same. Not ever.

Chapter Eighteen

Ashton tossed a rubber ball across the lawn to Buster and Bullwinkle and they chased after it.

"My dad's super angry that Stephanie got rid of his pool table while he's in Europe." Ashton tossed the ball again. "I heard her yelling at him on the phone late last night. She said he doesn't appreciate her and then she drove off in her Mercedes and didn't come back."

"Maybe she won't ever," I said.

"Yeah, I wish." Ashton lead the way to the pool room, where Consuela was setting out two glasses of lemonade and a plate of cookies for us.

"You look *bueno*!" she said when she saw me.

"*Muchos gracias*," I said, using my very best Spanish.

My dad had dropped me off at Ashton's house, and as we pulled into the circular driveway, he whistled when he saw the House That Looked Like a Hotel for the first time.

He shook his head. "I'm in the wrong line of business. Should have been a director. Could have filmed fake wars, not covered real ones, and made the big bucks!"

"Write your book, Dad." I kissed him on the cheek as I got out of his Range Rover.

"Maybe I will." He kissed me back. "Maybe I'll do just that."

Ashton and I practiced our scene for about an hour and high-fived each other when our rehearsal was over. We had nailed it and not messed up once. I knew Mr. Matheson would be happy. We spent the rest of the afternoon emailing everyone from school—teachers, parents, and kids in all grades—about our downtown adoption on Saturday. Ashton came up with the subject line: *In honor of Danny, the missing dog, come help us save others!*

"Rayleen picked up three more dogs in the past two days because of him," I said.

Ashton was lying on the floor with Buster and Bullwinkle slobbering all over him.

"Consuela says people who do good deeds get good things in return." Ashton rubbed his nose against Buster's flat one.

"People should do good deeds and expect nothing back," I said earnestly.

Ashton turned from his spot on the ground and looked at me. "Do you really believe that?"

"Yes, I do."

"Wow. That's amazing." Then he added softly, "Like you."

I blushed. "Why, thank you, King Oberon."

It was still light out when I got home, and I told my dad that I was going around the corner to check on Martha.

"Make sure you walk home before it gets dark, kiddo," he said as he watched me leave. My dad had a worried look on his face, and I knew it wasn't because I was walking alone down the street. He had just found out that he'd be leaving again on Monday to cover a story about a terrorist cell in Afghanistan. The fact that my mom was still so upset with me didn't make his leaving any easier, and although I had apologized to her over and over again, she was disconnected and distant toward me. I vowed I would never say anything that cruel to her again.

Martha came to the door when I knocked. She was wearing a yellow robe and slippers and apologized for not being dressed. She still looked pale, but at least she was up and walking around. The house smelled better and was cleaner, but it wasn't quite as fresh and polished-looking as it had been the first time I met her.

"I have the perfect solution for you," I said when we sat down.

"And what's that?" she said. Her voice still sounded scratchy and dry.

"I'm going to bring you someone to care for. Someone who really needs a lot of love and attention."

Martha's pale blue eyes brightened. "Well, I can't imagine," she said. Her bony hand went to her mouth and I could see the purple bruises where the IV needle had been inserted.

"His name's Neptune," I said, and took a breath. "He's a dog that got dumped at the shelter by his owner. He's sad and confused and needs someone kind and loving to take care of him."

Martha looked at me and shook her head.

"Bree, dear, that's awfully sweet of you, but I've

never had a dog. I'm not sure I'd know what to do with him."

"Feed him, care for him, give him love. I'll walk him for you," I added quickly, realizing that Neptune might be too much for her to walk on leash in her frail state.

"Well, I can barely take care of myself right now." She touched her hair, which clearly needed washing. "I don't think I'm up for this. . . ."

"Martha." I moved closer to her. "You said taking care of someone gave you a purpose."

She nodded slowly.

"Let Neptune be that someone," I said gently.

Martha ran her finger over a coaster on the table, which needed dusting. "Well, when you put it like that, let me think. . . ."

I felt my heart pounding inside my chest, like I was waiting for the results of a huge test. "He might be killed if we don't get him out in time," I said slowly.

Martha's eyes went wide. "Well, we can't have that, now can we? Why didn't you say so in the first place?"

"Martha." I looked into her watery blue eyes. "Are you saying yes?" Outside, people were taking their late afternoon walks to Ocean Avenue. Boys whizzed by on skateboards and cars came to a halt at stop signs. But inside a white-shuttered house on Marguerita Avenue at that exact moment, Martha took a step back into life.

"Yes, Bree." She smiled and folded her hands in her lap. "I am saying yes."

"Yippee! Hallelujah! Praise the gods above!" Rayleen whooped on the phone when I told her, "But listen, sweet pea, we're gonna have to show her the ropes, get the dog food, buy him a spanking new collar with her name and phone number on it, and make sure her yard's secure. I don't need another one gettin' out of a new home like Clay-man."

"I'll help her. I will."

"I know, sweet pea, but you've gotta know, there's a chance it won't work out. We're rollin' the big dice on this one: little old lady, big strong dog. Not usually the combo choice I'd make. If it doesn't work out . . ."

"I'll take Neptune." I said the words so fast I could barely believe I'd uttered them. "I can have two dogs. When Danny comes back, I'll just have them both."

Rayleen was silent for a moment. I heard her breathing against the receiver before she spoke again. "Good answer, sweet pea," she said. Then she hung up.

Chapter Nineteen

Neutrality: to be unengaged in a contest between others.
Omission: something left out or not done.
Fiasco: a complete disaster or failure.
Capitulate: to give up or surrender.
Tenable: ??
Stubborn: fixed or set in one's ways or opinions.

Those were the words on my vocab pop quiz the next day. Miss Jenson kept looking over at me since I kept looking up at the board hoping that the answers would miraculously appear.

"You won't find the answers there, Bree." She pointed to the board. "They're supposed to be in here."

She held an index finger against the side of her head. I had studied the words late last night and was having a problem remembering what "tenable" meant. I'd get a B if I missed it. I'd been so busy responding to emails and calls about the adoption event from total strangers and even a few teachers and students I barely knew who had promised to come. I also had to work out the details of getting Neptune to Martha. The paperwork was already done. It had been emailed to Martha and she had signed it and sent it back with her credit card number for the seventy-eight dollars it would cost to get him out. Neptune would be vet checked and given shots, neutered, and microchipped before he was released from the shelter. Rayleen and I had decided that it was best to take him to Martha late Saturday, after the event. That way we could spend time getting him settled. All of this, of course, had kept me from studying, and now I was facing the consequences.

Kate was sitting at a desk across the aisle from me, and she kept looking over at me, hoping I could telepathically give her the answers. She clearly hadn't studied hard enough either.

I looked at the word "tenable." I knew I had connected the answer to my mom while I was studying, but I couldn't remember why or how.

"You two need to make up properly before I leave on Monday," my dad had said as we sat through an uncomfortable dinner the night before.

"We'll be fine, Todd, stop worrying." The news-mom had given me a weak smile.

"Tenable" and Mom. I said it over and over in my head while Miss Jenson stood over my desk. Then it came to me. Manageable, workable, if not wonderful. We just had to get along reasonably well before my dad left. I quickly scribbled my answer. Done! Miss Jenson squinted down at my page, then nodded her head and moved on.

During recess, Ashton and I met in the drama lab. We had decided to get very professional and block the scene on the stage before we performed on Friday. We didn't have props yet—the art students were still working on them—and since we were supposed to be in the middle of a forest, Ashton insisted on using Mr. Matheson's small desk cactus to represent the whole woods. I had to laugh.

Ashton/King Oberon: "Ill met by moonlight, proud Titania."

Ashton came toward me and bowed deeply.

Me/QueenTitania: "What, jealous Oberon?—Fairies,

skip hence. I have forsworn his bed and company."

I spun on my heel and moved down stage left.

Ashton/King Oberon: "Tarry, rash wanton. Am not I thy lord?"

Ashton strode over to me and grabbed my hand and turned me to face him. I could feel his fingers smooth and soft against mine. This was the first time in rehearsal he had done this. Usually he tapped my shoulder and I turned around. I fumbled to find my next line as he kept my hand in his.

Me/Queen Titania: "Then I must be thy lady; but I know . . ."

My lines went clear out of my head as Ashton and I stood on the small stage facing each other.

"Sorry," I mumbled. "Let's start over again."

But Ashton didn't move. He looked at me in a way that no one had looked at me before. We stood so close I could see the yellow flecks around his hazel eyes. I felt my hand get clammy in his.

"I like you, Bree," he said softly. "You're not like all the other girls." He took my other hand.

We just stood there, staring at each other, not moving, fixed on each other, like nothing else in the world mattered in that moment.

"Bree! I've been looking eve—"

I turned quickly to see Kate, who had stopped dead

in her tracks in the drama lab doorway. Ashton let go of my hands and I felt myself turn red, purple, pink, and sickly green.

"Kate!" I said. "We're just rehearsing." I hurried over to her.

"So he is your boyfriend, like everyone is saying," she whispered. "I just saw you holding hands."

"It's part of the scene, okay? We're the king and queen."

"Don't they fight a lot? Seems like a weird interpretation." She frowned.

I looked back at Ashton, who was putting his copy of the play into his backpack.

Kate took a deep breath. "Look, Lulu texted me to say that you wouldn't be able to come to my birthday. Is it true?"

I took a deep breath. "Yes," I said. "I'm really sorry. I was going to . . ."

Ashton mumbled a quick good-bye as he brushed past us and headed out the door. I wanted to run after him to get him to come back so we could finish blocking the scene. More importantly, I wanted him to come back so I could tell him that I was really glad that he liked me, because I liked him, too. But I watched as he turned the corner down the hallway and was gone.

"Sorry." Kate shrugged. "Didn't mean to end your

rehearsal, but this couldn't wait."

"It's okay." I sighed.

"Well?" she asked, her big blue eyes growing wider.

"I'm putting on a big dog adoption day downtown. It had to be this Saturday. I have no choice. . . ."

"But it's my birthday." Kate's lower lip trembled. "We've been talking about it for months."

"I'll make it up to you. Promise," I said, and realized as she walked away that it was a line my mother had used on me many times.

Just as I was about to step into class I got a text message from Lulu, who was still out sick.

Did my Danny assignment. I called all the vets you emailed me. No luck.

Chapter Twenty

When I got home from school I called Ashton. His cell phone rang four times and then went to voice mail, so I tried his house. Consuela answered and when I asked for Ashton, she said he was busy, but she didn't sound very convincing. "You call back, okay? I tell him you want to speak with him," she said haltingly. I said I would try again but knew I wouldn't. Ashton was avoiding me and I wasn't sure why.

I walked around the house aimlessly and stopped at the sight of Danny's bed in the living room. The imprint that his body had made was no longer there and his food and water bowls had been removed from their place in the kitchen and put away in a cabinet. It was as if he were slowly disappearing from our lives, and soon there would be no sign that he had once lived here at all. I was filled with a pain so intense that it bit into every part of me like fierce red ants. I went over to Danny's comfy bed and curled up in it. I cried until it I felt like my ribs would break. When I was done, I just lay there for a long, long time.

Rayleen had left me a message on my cell phone while I was in class earlier telling me to write a note to Danny letting him know how much I missed him, and that when I was done I should put it in an envelope, seal it, and give it to her at our adoption event on Saturday. It sounded like a strange request, but once I eventually dragged myself out of Danny's doggy bed, it was the only thing I really wanted to do.

I took a blank piece of white paper out of the printer in my mom's office and sat at her desk and began writing.

To my dear dog Danny,

I can't believe it's been almost ten days since I last saw you. I pray that you will come back and I know in my heart that you're still alive. I hope that wherever you are you can feel how much you mean to me and that nothing would make me happier than to see your happy face looking up at me again.

I want you to know that I am sorry if you sometimes felt I used you to help me feel less lonely, but please know that you were never just a replacement for my parents being gone so much. I also want you to know that in the last ten days I met a wonderful woman named Rayleen who has truly helped me to understand dogs in a way I never did before. I have so much more to tell you, but most importantly, I just want you to know that you are missed beyond words and I love you with all my heart.

Be safe and come back soon. PLEASE!

XOXO,

Bree

I folded the letter and put it in an envelope and sealed it like Rayleen had asked me to do. Somehow writing the letter had made me feel better, like Danny was just a bit closer than before.

I sat in the living room and went over my lines for *A Midsummer Night's Dream* one last time before our performance the next day. I felt a knot in my stomach when I got to Ashton's line, "Tarry, rash wonton. Am not I thy lord?" I remembered how his hand had felt in mine.

My mom's attitude, surprisingly, had actually been better when she'd picked me up after school earlier. She had asked me a few questions about the downtown adoption day in a very neutral voice. She'd wanted to know what Steve the New Hope coordinator's last name was, and I told her it was Samuels. I shared with her that I wanted to get the twenty-eight red listed dogs adopted by the end of the day, and as many more dogs as we could. The newsmom asked a few other questions, then dropped me off without a kiss, but with a small wave good-bye before she raced back to the station.

Just as I was finishing the rest of my homework, the gate phone rang. I was a little startled since I wasn't expecting any visitors. I was never allowed to let anyone in if I was alone in the house, even if they said they were delivery people or worked for the electric company or something like that. The newsparents had drilled it into me so many times, but I knew it was just their way of making sure I stayed safe.

"Who is it?" I asked.

"It's Rayleen, sweet pea, let me in."

There was no mistaking Rayleen's singsong southern

twang, and no one but her ever called me sweet pea, so I was pretty certain it was safe to buzz her in.

"Lookin' a little puffy-eyed there," Rayleen said as I opened the door. She never missed anything. She was dressed in her usual style: flip-flops and cargo pants with a T-shirt that said "Underdogs to Top Dogs."

"Cool T-shirt," I said.

She opened a large canvas bag that was slung over her shoulder and took out an identical T-shirt. "Knew you'd want one." She grinned. "Lil' present from me. Wear it on Saturday." She tossed the T-shirt over to me.

"Thanks." I held it against me. "I love it!"

"Take a look at what's on the back." Rayleen turned around.

Written across it in bold blue letters were the words "Save a shelter dog. Mutts are miracles." I went to her and gave her a big hug.

"I have a whole bunch for the volunteers to wear. Thought it might help adopt a dog or two. Seeing your clever words on the banner outside will be great, but having a reminder inside the shelter can't hurt."

"That's brilliant!" I said, and gave her another hug. It was so easy to be warm to Rayleen. Why couldn't I be that way with the newsmom? I didn't have time to dwell on the matter because Rayleen was in high gear.

"I've got a carload of dog stuff for Martha. Thought

we could run it over now and get everything set up. Also, I wanna check her fences to make sure there's no way out for our big boy."

I called Martha and she said it was fine for us to come over.

On the short drive to Marguerita Avenue, Rayleen made me make her a promise. If everything worked out with Neptune and Martha, that would be great, but she reminded me that Martha was an old lady and Neptune was only a two-year-old dog. "There might come a time when you'll need to take Neptune. I don't ever want him back in a shelter again, or in the hands of the wrong owner."

"I promise, but you'll be around, won't you?" I said just as we pulled up outside Martha's house.

Rayleen turned to look at me with her wide-set green eyes. "Prob'ly not, sweet pea. I never stay too long in one place." She turned from me quickly and pulled the key from the ignition and hopped out.

I sat there for a moment, unmoving. Rayleen had just come into my life. I couldn't stand the thought of her leaving already. I had learned so much from her and felt so close to her. I had pictured us going to the shelter and saving dogs together for years and years. I couldn't bear the thought of not hearing her voice or breathing in her special scent. But Rayleen didn't give me time to sit there and mope. She came around to my side of the truck and made a silly, monkey-looking face and motioned for me to get out. I laughed. She was the one person who somehow, no matter what, managed to make me laugh.

We carried a huge dog bed, dog bowls, and dog food up the pathway and knocked on Martha's front door.

"It's the shelter Santas!" I yelled though the door when Martha asked who was there.

Martha opened the door and I was happy to see that she was dressed in a skirt and top and had a touch of pink lipstick on. I did the introductions, and Martha grew more excited with each thing Rayleen showed her.

"This must be what it feels like to be waiting for a new baby to arrive," she said, smoothing down her skirt, her eyes bright and clear and focused on everything we had brought.

"Well, consider this the baby shower, then," Rayleen said.

When we were done setting up the bowls in the kitchen, the dog bed in the living room, and had put all the dog food away, Martha took us out to the back garden. Rayleen gave a long, low whistle when she saw how big it was.

"Wow. A dog's paradise. He sure is one lucky boy to call this place his home."

Rayleen walked every inch of the garden and checked for possible holes or spaces where Neptune might be able to get out, but didn't find anything that concerned her.

"My husband, Tim, he took such pride in the garden," Martha said.

"He did a beautiful job." Rayleen took in the roses that were in full bloom everywhere.

"I've got a gardener coming once a week now to do the heavy stuff, Bree. It was just too much for me to do on my own. I can putter about on the weekends, that's fine. Neptune can help me plant my first project. A vegetable garden."

"I'm sure he's great at digging holes," Rayleen said, and winked at me.

My cell phone rang and I answered it quickly, hoping it was Ashton, but it was my dad. He had come home to find me gone. I'd forgotten to leave a note.

"I was worried, kiddo."

"I'm sorry, Dad. I'm just down the road with Rayleen. . . ."

"It's getting late. Time to come back and start your homework," he said gently but firmly.

I told Rayleen we'd better get going.

* * *

Martha had picked some roses and handed them to us at the door. "Special flowers for two special ladies."

We thanked her and said our good-byes.

When Rayleen dropped me off, she gave me a big thumbs-up as she drove away. I watched as her car got smaller and smaller as she headed down our street. I couldn't stand the idea that soon she'd be gone.

"I'm home!" I shouted as I closed the front door behind me.

My dad was sitting in the living room, working on his laptop. He looked up when I came into the room. A crease formed between his eyebrows.

"Look, kiddo, I know how important animals are to you, but you've got to make sure you get your homework done, too. Rayleen's a great person, but you're spending a lot of time with her."

"She's leaving soon, so you don't have to worry about her for much longer."

He seemed taken aback.

"Where's she going?

"I don't know. Wherever the wind takes her, I guess," I said softly.

My dad was silent, then spoke. "I'm sorry she's leaving. Honest." He drummed his fingers on the top of his laptop. “I wish I didn’t have to leave again so soon.”

“Stay home and write your book,” I said. “I wish you would, Daddy.”

My dad stood up and came over to me and wrapped his arms around me. “If only it were that simple, kiddo.” He pulled me in close, his words catching in the back of his throat.

I went upstairs to help him pack for his trip to Afghanistan. He wasn’t leaving for a few days, but he wanted to get the packing done so he didn’t have to think about it. He would be gone for a month or longer. I knew that where he was going was remote and dangerous and I wouldn’t get to talk to him very often. This would probably be the only time we had alone together before he left. While we folded shirts and rolled socks, I asked him lots of questions about the book he wanted to write.

He stopped to think for a moment. Then it all poured out of him in one breath.

“From all my travels and experiences around the world I’ve learned that no matter how different people and cultures are, basically, human beings all want the same things. Love and acceptance. Wars are just a nasty way of trying to get those needs met, and mankind needs to find an alternative solution. I’d like to write a book about the better way."

"Wow, Dad. That sounds awesome! It's going to be a great book for sure."

"Thanks, but I have to find the time to write it first." He sighed, then went into his walk-in closet to get more clothes.

While I was folding his crisp, button-down shirts, my cell phone beeped. I had a text message. It was from Ashton.

Sorry I've been MIA. My dad came home to deal with Stephanie. Total chaos. She broke a bunch of stuff when she left and yelled at Consuela, who's crying in the kitchen now.

Wow, I wrote back. *Good news about Stephanie. Sorry about Consuela. That sucks. How r u?*

Much better, he wrote back.

I am too, I wanted to say, *since you wrote.* But of course I didn't.

I tossed and turned in bed all night. I was nervous about the play and equally nervous about the adoption event on Saturday. I hated that my dad was leaving for so long and that Rayleen wouldn't be around much longer. I was sad that Lulu wouldn't be showing up at adoption day since I had insisted she go to Kate's party. I was feeling left out of the fun spa day all the girls in my class would have, despite the fact that I knew my adoption day was really important.

And then there were my mom and Danny. It felt like I had lost them both. Would either of them ever come back to me?

Chapter Twenty-One

Mr. Matheson had said that we didn't need to wear real costumes, but we could bring things from home or pick symbolic items that revealed something about our character for our performances. Since I was a queen, the first thing I decided on was a crown. I had to dig it out from the back of my closet and I hoped it hadn't gotten crushed under shoe boxes and Rollerblades. I had worn it a few Halloweens ago when I decided to be Glinda, the Good Witch of the North. Luckily, the crown was intact and still sparkled. I choose a red dress that I'd worn to a Christmas party at my mom's TV station last year. Although I knew it was a bit dressy for school and I'd be stuck in it all day, I wanted to look as queenly as I could.

I guess I hadn't taken into account that red velvet should be worn only at one time of the year—Christmas.

"Where's Ashton the red-nosed reindeer?" some kid said as I walked into class. I didn't look back to see who it was.

My face was as red as my dress as I made my way to the back of the drama lab.

"Our queen has arrived!" Mr. Matheson announced as I hurried to my seat. "And looking quite royal and regal, I might add."

I gave him a weak, less than queenly smile.

Mr. Matheson had the tips of his hair spiked white today, while the rest of his hair was black. Black and white. That's how things were supposed to be. Clear and defined. Black or white. But most things in life, it seemed, were gray.

Would Ashton and I still be close after this? Answer? Gray.

Would Danny come back? Answer? Gray.

To be, or not to be. Shakespeare's own words. Answer? Gray.

I sat at my desk and wrote in my notebook,

"No more gray. Except when I'm old and gray, like Martha."

I looked around the drama lab for Ashton. His sidekick, Max, was already in his seat, so where was he? Come to think of it, I hadn't seen him at all yet today.

Mr. Matheson must have read my mind because he looked around and said with a slightly flustered look on his face, "Where, pray tell, is King Ashton?"

"In the nurse's office. Feeling sick," Max said.

I felt my hands get icy cold. I wondered what was wrong with him.

"Well, then, class, we'll start the performances with the Helena and Lysander scene." He turned to me. "Queen Titania, wilt thou to yonder nurse's office and find out what ails the king?"

Everyone laughed.

As I made my way to the door I had to walk past Kate, who was getting ready to go onstage to play Helena. "Good luck," I said as I passed by.

"Thanks," she said, but she still seemed upset with me. She had on a beautiful cape that was covered with multicolored flowers, which looked almost real. I was sorry I was going to miss her performance.

I walked into the nurse's office and announced that I was there to see Ashton. The school nurse was a short, squat, no-nonsense, middle-aged woman whose name I could never remember since everyone at school just called her "nurse."

"He's got a bad stomachache." She gave me a quick once-up-and-down, taking in my velvet dress and crown, which I had forgotten was already perched on the top of my head.

"Well, nurse, you see, Mr. Matheson sent me to get Ashton. He's supposed to be performing now in drama lab."

"That'll explain the fancy gold medallion he's wearing around his neck," she said with a snort.

"May I see him?"

She waved her stubby hand in the direction of the sick room door.

The sick room had two folding cots and a rollaway table in it. There wasn't much in terms of medical supplies except for a thermometer and one of those armband things that takes your blood pressure. In a cabinet they kept Band-Aids and alcohol swabs, but not a whole lot else. It was more of a way station until a parent arrived to pick you up.

I knocked softly, then pushed the sick room door open. Ashton was curled up with his back to me. His gold medallion, which was very large, hung over his shoulder and was all that I could see, since he was facing the wall.

"Ashton, it's Bree. Can I come in?"

He rolled over onto his back and put a hand up over his forehead.

"Yeah, sure," he said, keeping his eyes closed.

"What's wrong?" I asked, walking gingerly over to the cot.

"Everything." He sniffed. "I didn't sleep last night and I've got a bad stomachache."

"I'm sorry." I wanted to touch him on his arm to let him know I really cared, but I held myself in check. "We're supposed to be performing right now," I said softly.

"Oh, no! I fell asleep in here during first period. I woke up when you came in." He sat up suddenly, then groaned and clutched his stomach.

"You look terrible!" I said. "Lie down."

He looked at me in my red dress and crown.

"You look really nice." He gave me a crooked smile then lay back down.

I was glad that he wasn't still looking at me, because I could feel my cheeks getting fiery hot.

"Does your dad know you're sick?"

"Nah. Left this morning. He's already on a plane back to Europe."

"Do you think you can get up?"

"I'm sorry, Bree. I just can't perform right now." He

held a hand over his eyes.

"It's okay," I said, but swallowed hard. We had rehearsed so much and had done so well. I knew we were going to nail our performance today, and now we weren't even going to get a shot at it.

"Last night was terrible," Ashton said suddenly. "Stephanie and my dad were screaming at each other for, like, hours. Then she started throwing anything and everything she could, and my dad threatened to call the police. Buster and Bullwinkle went berserk because of all the noise, so my dad made me lock them in my room. Consuela started crying and wouldn't stop. Then at about three A.M., my dad came to my bedroom and told me it might be best if I move to New York to live with my mom."

"You can't!" I blurted out. "You just can't," I said softer. First Rayleen, now Ashton. I couldn't bear the thought of another person I cared about leaving.

Ashton sighed. "Thanks. Glad someone wants me around. Don't worry, my mom isn't up for having me and the hound dogs. It would cramp her busy social life."

I felt myself exhale slowly with relief.

"I'm sorry about everything," I said, thinking he was far worse off than I was in terms of a mother. At least mine was around some of the time.

I told Ashton not to worry about the performance and to get some rest and I'd explain everything to Mr. Matheson. I wanted to ask him if he thought he'd be up for adoption day tomorrow but thought better of it. He had enough to recover from with last night's events in his perfect house, which was, I now knew, far from perfect.

I ended up performing the part of Queen Titania, but it wasn't with my first choice king. Instead, Mr. Matheson took on the role of King Oberon. We got through it okay, with him reading the lines from the book and me doing my very best to block out the voice of Ashton speaking the king's part. I had to fight back disappointment and not miss a single gesture or word, and I tried not to wince when Mr. Matheson spun me around to face him when he said, "Tarry, rash wanton. Am not I thy lord?"

"Bravo!" Mr. Matheson bowed and applauded me when it was over and the rest of the class followed suit.

Kate gave me a hug and said I did an awesome job, but despite the fact that I knew I'd probably get an A, I felt incredibly empty, like a balloon that had just had all the air let out.

Chapter Twenty-Two

When I got home that afternoon I had what seemed like a million emails about the adoption day. People wanted to know if they would be allowed to take the dog they adopted that day. My answer back was yes, if the dog was already spayed or neutered and microchipped and given all its shots. If the dog still had to be neutered or spayed, the pickup would be a day or so later. Any questions about adoption fees and dog licenses I forwarded to New Hope Steve, as I had affectionately started calling him. We emailed each other at least once a day with updates. If half the people who said they were going to come showed up, there would be a big crowd at the shelter tomorrow. Steve had started calling me "Bree the Great," because he said I was just that.

There were also a few more "Found Danny" emails, but I had lost the excited, anxious feeling I got when I read about each dog and opened the picture attachments. I knew none of them would be him. And they weren't. I forwarded those emails to Rayleen, who was doing a great job finding fosters and homes for the Danny dogs. I was trying very hard not to give up hope with each day that passed, but I was still filled with dread that he was gone forever. I had put the letter that Rayleen had asked me to write to Danny in the canvas tote bag that I was taking with me downtown tomorrow. I had also packed my digital camera, knowing that I wanted to have adoption day recorded and saved for all time.

While I was finishing replying to the last of my emails, my dad put his head into my room and announced that the three of us were going out to dinner at my mom's favorite Greek restaurant in Malibu.

"I know you've got an early start tomorrow, Bree, but I want to make this a special dinner with my two girls before I leave."

How could I say no?

We drove down Pacific Coast Highway with the

sun casting shimmering golden light across the ocean. I watched as the glowing ball inched its way over the horizon and closed my eyes, like I always did just as it disappeared, and wished.

"Please let us adopt all the red listed dogs and some of the others, and please, please bring Danny back to me."

I opened my eyes to see that my mom had turned around and was staring at me. There was an expression on her face I had never seen before. She looked different, softer, and was focused intently on me. Then I realized what it was. The newsmom was, in that moment, completely still.

"Friends?" she asked quietly.

I sat there staring at her, not saying a word. I wanted more than anything to feel close to her, but she flip-flopped on me all the time. My mom was never consistent. There was only one thing that was truly consistent about her: she was always busy.

Dinner at the Greek Taverna started out with thick, rich lentil soup and warm bread served on the casual red-and-white patio tables. My dad told us more about the political strife and government problems in Afghanistan, and my mom asked me all about how the scene in drama lab with Ashton had gone. I shared a few details and she seemed genuinely upset to hear that Ashton hadn't been able to perform with me. But near the end of dinner, over the delicious, rich baklava that was the restaurant's most popular dessert, my mom reached over and touched my arm.

"Bree, honey. You know I'm really going to try and be there tomorrow. Dad will be there for sure, and I'm going to make every effort."

"I understand, Mom." I looked at her. "Work comes first." I thought about how I was disappointing Kate tomorrow and how my mom might have to disappoint me. "You can't be in two places at once. I get it."

A look passed between my mom and dad. I was usually pretty good at reading the newsparents' silent communication, but for once I had a hard time deciphering it.

"That's very big of you, kiddo," my dad said.

My mom reached over and squeezed my hand.

"I'm really going to try to be there."

On the drive back home I could see the Santa Monica Pier lights twinkling in the distance and the Ferris wheel at the end of the boardwalk going around and around on its never-ending circular journey. I wished I was high up on it, spinning effortlessly in the cool, dark night sky. Above the world where people disappointed and hurt one another. I wanted to be far away, in a place where animals didn't suffer and weren't abandoned. A place where friendships lasted forever and parents understood that being there for their kids was all that we ever wanted.

"Why so quiet?" my dad asked as the electric gates to our home swung open.

"Thinking," I said.

"Good thoughts, I hope," my mother said as she got out of the car and made her way up the steps to our house. I followed.

Chapter Twenty-Three

I barely slept a wink all night, but at seven A.M. I was awake and dressed in my "Underdogs to Top Dogs" T-shirt and a pair of jeans that were now reserved strictly for the shelter. Rayleen picked me up an hour later.

She played Elvis's "Hound Dog" about five times in the car and made me sing along loudly with her, like a coach pumping her team up before the big game.

"Don't sell too hard, sweet pea. Let people show interest in the animal first before you jump in and give 'em a hundred reasons why this is the greatest dog in the world for them. Let 'em feel the spirit of the dog, even though the shelter often brings out fear in 'em and they're not their shining best. We've set up a few extra private play yards so the potential new owners can get some private time away from all the yapping and barking." Rayleen babbled at top speed and drove that way, too. We reached the shelter in record time.

It was all the brightly colored balloons that I first saw. They were tied to every pole and tree and door handle outside the normally gray, plain building.

"Steve's idea." Rayleen smiled as we pulled into the still almost empty parking lot. "He wanted it to look extra special for you. He thinks you're—"

"The greatest." I laughed. "I know. Well, I hope he still thinks so by the end of today."

"Close your eyes," Rayleen instructed as we walked in the direction of the entrance. She crooked her arm through mine and led me up the steps until we were standing right at the top, in front of the main entrance doors. "Now open 'em!"

I opened my eyes and felt an overwhelming desire to shout with joy and cry at the same time. Hanging over the entrance was a huge white banner that said in giant blue letters, "Save a shelter dog. Mutts are miracles," as we had discussed, but the words that were written in a slightly smaller font below that were completely unexpected. "Adoptions today in honor of Bree and her dog,

Danny." I turned to Rayleen, who put her arms around me as my eyes welled with tears.

"It's okay. You're allowed," she said. I breathed in her wet earth and lavender scent. "Made me cry last night when Steve and I put it up." She sniffed, as if she were ready to start again herself.

"It's the nicest thing anyone's ever done for me." I wiped my eyes with the back of my hand.

"The note," Rayleen said softly, "the one you wrote to Danny." She held out her hand and I fished it out of my canvas bag.

"What are you going to do with it?" I asked.

She looked at me with her green eyes. "Make sure he gets it," she said, and tucked it into the back pocket of her jeans.

The morning went by in a frenzy of dog baths, nail clippings, bows being tied on necks, and cages being cleaned and then cleaned again.

All the volunteers and staff were given the special "Underdogs to Top Dogs" T-shirts to wear once the spruce-up was complete. One of the volunteers had baked two huge tubs full of crunchy biscuits, and the dogs each got to have one before the doors were opened to the general public. The shelter dogs must have felt the excitement, because there was lots of yapping and barking, but for once they sounded happier and less desperate, as if they somehow knew there was something special going on today.

I checked on Neptune, who had been bathed and had a gold ribbon around his neck. He looked like a prince. I patted him on his smooth back and looked into his sad eyes.

"Prince Neptune, today's the day your new life begins."

Neptune, of course, had an "adopted" notation hanging on his cage door so everyone would know he was spoken for. Martha had called me twice already this morning, and I had promised her we would have him delivered by six P.M. at the latest.

I was so focused on getting everything ready that I totally forgot to worry about Ashton coming. The only thing that really mattered to me right now was the dogs.

"I just checked and there's a big crowd out there," New Hope Steve, who was also wearing the special T-shirt, told the twenty-three staff and volunteers who had gathered together in the office before the main doors were opened. "Let's give a big round of applause to the girl who made this day happen. To Bree the Great!" he shouted.

I was standing next to Rayleen, and she had to put

her hand out to steady me. All eyes were on me, and everyone smiled and looked at me with such kindness and support. These people had all been total strangers to me until just recently, and now they were like my special family. We were all united by a common goal and cause. I applauded them back as hugs and kisses went all around.

"Showtime!" Steve said, and jangled the keys to the shelter's entrance.

Just before the doors opened I checked my phone. There was a message from Ashton saying that he was so sorry, but he really was sick and in bed at home, and he'd check in with me later to see how it went. He wished me luck. I had another message from Lulu. It said, "I'm outside! Let me in!" I felt a rush of warmth for her. We'd have to make it up to Kate with a special "birthday for three" night next week. I hoped she'd understand.

It is hard to describe how incredible I felt seeing the familiar faces of parents and kids from school, as well as teachers like Mr. Matheson and even the school nurse. The nurse! Apparently she wanted a small dog to keep her company in her apartment in Encino, and I found her the perfect one. A red listed, seven-year-old poodle that needed lots of love and care. She seemed thrilled with him. There were families that arrived with carloads of children and couples looking for a dog for the first time. There was a silver-haired woman who cried nonstop because her fifteen-year-old dog had died last week and she was ready to give another one love. I matched her with a red listed German shepherd who was shy and had come in as a stray. Lulu got into the swing of things right away and discovered she had a knack for calming down a biting Chihuahua who had been listed as "unadoptable."

"I'm calling my mom. I want him!" Lulu yelled as I walked by the cage, where she was sitting on the floor holding him.

Rayleen came to find me in one of the play yards, where I was helping a young couple with an overweight Bassett hound who had been severely neglected by his past owners and was also red listed. "Your dad's here. He's in the entrance." I excused myself and let Rayleen take over.

I walked through the din of barking dogs and the groups of people walking the aisles looking into the cages. I was happy to see that a number of them were already empty. Rayleen had moved Neptune to the inside office holding cage because so many people had been interested in him and were disappointed to learn that he was already adopted. As I checked in on him, curled up and asleep on a blanket, I flashed back to the day that I had watched him get dropped off and abandoned by his owner. Now, freedom and a new beginning were just a few hours away for him.

I turned to see Officer Reyes standing behind me.

"I've been telling Neptune here what a lucky dog he is." Officer Reyes smiled warmly at me. "What you've done here today, Bree . . . incredible." He held his arms wide-open as if they were encompassing the whole shelter. Then he paused. "You've given me back something I'm ashamed to say I'd lost a few years back. You don't need to place all the red listed dogs to win our bet. You've won it already."

I stood and turned to face him. "No, Officer Reyes, it's not me who has won. It's the animals. They'll be glad to have you back."

As I approached the entrance I saw my dad standing and talking to New Hope Steve. I was filthy, with muddy paw prints up and down my T-shirt, and a grimy doggy lick or two had probably left its mark on my face, but I didn't care.

My dad stood and stared at me. I guess I looked pretty bad, but then he smiled.

"Bree," he said, giving me a hug. "I was just telling Steve here how proud of you I am. This is wonderful!"

"She's the greatest, sir. Wish there were more kids like her." Steve flashed me a white smile.

"Well, is the Davies family adopting a new dog today, Bree?" my dad asked cautiously.

I felt a lump in my throat, as if I had swallowed a marble.

"No, Dad. We're not. I'm waiting for Danny."

Steve and my dad gave each other a look I definitely understood. It was one of pity. Something I never wanted from anyone. Before I had a chance to say anything back, there was a commotion outside. Loud voices could be heard as a van backed up to the entrance to the shelter.

One of the volunteers came running over to Steve. "The press is here!"

"Go find Rayleen," Steve instructed the volunteer, who scurried through the back of the shelter. I text messaged Lulu quickly and told her to come out front.

Steve, my dad, and I went outside. The crowd had gathered around the cameraman, who was trying to pan a shot of the huge banner and then get close-ups of people leaving with their newly adopted pets. There was a group blocking the news van, so I couldn't tell which channel had decided to cover our event. But when the cameraman zoomed in on the reporter who had just begun speaking, I didn't have to wonder which channel it was anymore. Lulu and Rayleen reached me simultaneously. I stood there with one of them on each side, unable to breathe or move as I watched the perfectly groomed woman in the all-too-familiar cream suit.

"This is Colleen Davies with Channel Five reporting from the downtown Vox Street Animal Shelter, where a most special adoption day is happening inside."

I felt my dad put his arm on me from behind. "She wouldn't have missed this for the world," he said into my ear.

Rayleen looked over and gave me a wink.

"It's your mom!" Lulu said.

The world moved in slow motion, as if time somehow knew that this was a moment so precious to me that I needed to hold on to it second by second. Word by word. Frame by frame.

The newsmom held up a picture of Danny, the same one that we had on the flyers, and the cameraman zoomed in close on his face as my mom continued.

"This event was inspired by a dog named Danny, who was recently lost in Santa Monica. He has yet to be found, but in his young owner's search to find him, she discovered the world of animal shelters." My mom held my gaze for a second. "That young owner just happens to be my very own, very special twelve-year-old daughter, Bree." My mom's voice wavered, but being the professional reporter that she was, she quickly pulled herself together and continued. "The Humane Society of the United States estimates that more than three million dogs and cats are euthanized in shelters in the United States every year. This young girl decided that she could make a difference and try to help save some of the LA shelter dogs. In an interview yesterday with the shelter's New Hope coordinator, Steve Samuels, I learned that the goal today was for all red listed dogs—meaning dogs set to be euthanized on Monday—to be adopted today, and Steve just sent me a quick message that the last of those twenty-eight dogs has just been adopted." The cameraman zoomed in close on the young couple leaving with the overweight basset hound.

The growing crowd applauded.

Rayleen and Lulu each put their arms around me.

"This is way better than a spa day!" Lulu whispered.

"Told you your mama loved you," Rayleen said, her voice breaking on the word "mama." I knew how much she missed hers.

"While Danny might never be found, he certainly has helped to save others," my mom said as she wrapped up.

The cameraman zoomed in close again on Danny's picture and gave my mom the thumbs-up with his free hand before lowering his camera.

The newsmom just stood there, her mic in one hand and the picture of Danny in the other. She looked small and lost suddenly as she turned to look at me, her eyes filled with tears.

"Go to her, Bree," my dad whispered.

I ran to her and felt her soft blouse crush against me. I held on to her, neither of us caring that the dirt would ruin her suit and she'd have to change for the next shot.

"I love you." She stroked my hair.

"I love you back," I said, and really, truly meant it.

"I've lost you for too long," she whispered against my hair. "And now that I've got you back, I'm never, ever going to let you go again. Okay?"

"Okay, Mom." I held on to her even tighter. "Okay."

Rayleen let out one of her famous loud whistles while Steve, Lulu, and my dad applauded.

The newsmom did change out of her now dirt-stained suit, but into something she normally wouldn't wear on camera. She put on one of our "Underdogs to Top Dogs" T-shirts and interviewed me and Rayleen and a whole bunch of people who were adopting dogs, as well as a few of the staff and volunteers. She had great footage of Steve from the interview she had secretly done with him already. Sneaky Steve was his new nickname, but I loved him for it.

At four o'clock, when the adoption event was over, the newsmom did one last take, standing in front of now empty cages, their doors swung wide open. "This is Colleen Davies from Channel Five leaving you with one last thought. Please give these deserving animals a chance and adopt from your local shelters."

My mom had to leave with her crew, and my dad was taking Lulu home. Lulu had convinced her parents to let her bring home the biting Chihuahua, who she had already named Taz.

"Let's hope he likes horses," she said as she hugged me good-bye.

All of us who were left cleaned up, and then it was time to get Neptune and take him to his new home. Rayleen put a brand-new collar on him with a tag that had both mine and Martha's phone numbers. She fastened a leather leash to his choke chain and, after saying our good-byes, we walked through the entrance to the outside.

"Wait!" Rayleen stopped at the threshold. "Put your right paw out first." She positioned Neptune's right paw out the door. "Gotta start out on the right foot, big boy." He looked up at her with a slightly bewildered look but did what she wanted.

It was almost unbelievable to watch the transformation in Neptune the moment he was out of the shelter. His tail started wagging as soon as he breathed in fresh air. He sat looking over my shoulder and drooling on my neck all the way back to Santa Monica.

I text messaged Ashton while we were driving. *Great Day. All red listed dogs adopted plus eighteen more. Watch Channel Five news at six. My mom covered the event. Hope u feel better.*

I knew today was a day I would never forget, and it had been wonderful in almost every way. The shelter dogs had found new owners and lucky people now had loyal, loving pets. And my mom and I were on the way to being the way we always should have been.

But there was a hole inside me that could not be filled. A member of our family was still absent.

Danny.

Chapter Twenty-Four

"Look, he's smelling the roses!" Martha said as we all watched Neptune prance around the backyard. It had been love at first sight, with Neptune giving Martha big doggy kisses as she knelt down beside him and put her arms around his neck. It was like he had always belonged there.

Once we had shown Neptune where his doggy bowls and bed were, we'd taken him outside. Rayleen had to stop Neptune from jumping on Martha since she was so small and he was so big, but she quickly corrected that problem with a spray bottle filled with water.

"You spray him quickly in the face once, pretty soon he'll just see the bottle and not jump," Rayleen explained.

"He is one gorgeous animal," Martha marveled as Neptune stretched out on the patio in the sun. He had spent the past hour racing around the garden and catching the ball that we had bought for him. Martha had cooked a big pot of chicken, yams, and rice for him, and he had gobbled it down ravenously. Rayleen and I had brought him a big meat bone to chew on, and Martha had walked to the Montana Avenue pet store and bought him expensive dog treats. Exhausted, happy, and full, he lay sleeping in the sun.

"Tim would have loved him." Martha sighed. "He always wanted a big dog, but I always said no. Now I have the very thing he always wanted."

"Don't you fret about past regrets. That's what my mama always said." Rayleen patted her on the arm.

"You're right." Martha nodded. "There's a saying that goes, 'Yesterday is history. Tomorrow is a mystery. And today? Today is a gift. That's why we call it the present.'"

"The gift today is Neptune," I said.

Neptune yawned and looked up at us at the sound

of his name. His amber eyes took us all in. It had been a group effort of three—Martha, Rayleen, and me—and now here he was, stretched out in a beautiful backyard, starting his peaceful new life.

"The new man of the house." Martha smiled, gazing at him in wonderment. "Lazy, but very handsome."

We all laughed.

My cell phone rang just as we were heading indoors for some tea and sandwiches that Martha had made for us. It was my home number and I hoped my mom and dad weren't angry because I had been at Martha's much longer than I had told them.

"Bree, come home now!" my mom yelled.

"I'm sorry, I—"

"No, you don't understand." She sounded like she was having a hard time catching her breath. "We got a call at the station. Bree, I think Danny's been found!"

"No, Mom. I get emails all the time. They just look—"

"Bree! What's Martha's address again? Dad and I are getting in the car now. We've got to get to Sherman Oaks."

"Sherman Oaks? That's miles from here!"

"Bree, the address!"

I told her the house number and hung up the phone. I felt numb. I wouldn't allow myself to get my hopes up again like I had so many times in the past few weeks, from Martha's call about Danny's collar to chasing Clay down the alleyways believing it was him and clicking on picture after picture of dogs that weren't Danny. I couldn't let myself do it again.

"What's wrong, sweet pea?" Rayleen asked.

I sat down on the couch in a daze.

"You're white as a sheet," Martha said with concern.

"My mom just called." I could barely get the words out. "She says Danny's been found."

Martha let out a hoot. "Well you should be jumping up and down for joy, young lady."

Rayleen sat down next to me and took my hand in hers.

"Bree, look at me." I turned and held her steady gaze. "I know you don't trust that it's really him, and I understand." She squeezed my fingers tight. "But it is, sweet pea. I promise."

I heard my dad's Range Rover honking outside and I jumped up quickly and raced out the door before even saying good-bye.

"Call when you have him!" Rayleen yelled after me.

I jumped into the backseat and my dad put the car into a screeching reverse.

"What happened?" I asked, barely able to get the words past the tightness in my chest.

As we raced along Sunset Boulevard toward the 405 freeway, my mom filled me in.

"The station got a phone call right after the segment aired at six o'clock. A man called saying that after seeing the picture of Danny on the news, he was sure it was the injured dog he and his wife had found lying on the side of the road on Mulholland Drive a few weeks ago."

"Injured?" I said as a knot tightened in my stomach.

"The station reached me at once and I called the man right back to get the whole story," my mom said breathlessly.

"Apparently he was hit by a car. Broken leg," my dad chimed in quickly.

"Oh, no!" I felt my stomach lurch as my dad sped down the freeway toward the Ventura Boulevard exit.

"He must have run a long way. Dogs sometimes do that. They found him close to the entrance of your school, Bree," my mom continued.

I flashed back to Danny jumping out of the car when my mom picked me up from school.

"Eight miles from home. That's crazy," I said softly.

"Well, this kind man and his wife were driving to their home in Sherman Oaks along Mulholland Drive and saw this dog lying on the side of the road. He couldn't walk, so they put him in their car and rushed him to their vet. They have two dogs of their own and knew what to do. Their vet scanned him but found no microchip, and he didn't have a collar either."

"It came off in Santa Monica, by Martha's house," I said.

"They posted Found Dog signs, but none that we would have seen."

"The vet had to reset his leg and has kept him confined in a cage at his facility," my dad said.

I thought of all the dogs I had seen in cages at the shelter, and how often I had imagined Danny stuck in a cage where I would never find him again.

"George and his wife—those are the people who found him—decided that if they couldn't locate the owners once his leg healed, they would turn him over to a rescue group."

"I still don't believe it's him. It's not possible," I said as we pulled up outside the Sherman Oaks Veterinary Group.

My dad switched off the ignition and turned back to me.

"Rayleen said he'd be back when the time was right. Remember?"

I nodded.

My dad smiled. "It's time."

* * *

We were met in the vet's waiting room by a balding, older man with soft brown eyes. His redheaded wife wore a sweater embossed with Pomeranians on it.

"These are our dogs. I knitted it myself," she said after my mom and dad introduced themselves to George and Verna, the couple who had found the dog—I refused to say Danny. I had been through too many disappointments already.

"We're so grateful," my mom said. "Thank you."

As we sat in the vet's lobby, I felt my heart pounding hard against my chest. The receptionist told us to wait and that Dr. Shapiro would be out in a minute.

As my parents made small talk with Verna and George, a wave of emotions washed over me. It was as if all that I had been through since Danny had disappeared hit me at once like a tidal wave. Disbelief, sadness, hurt, anger, disappointment, fear, anticipation, exhaustion, and joy. Yes, joy for all the animals I had helped save. But there was still an emptiness inside me.

"Please, please be Danny." I closed my eyes and prayed as the gray-haired vet in the white lab coat came out to get us.

It's hard to explain those minutes when we followed Dr. Shapiro down the corridor that smelled like disinfectant and sat and waited, yet again, in an examining room. Dr. Shapiro said that the border collie was doing much better. He had come in very hungry and dehydrated, most likely from being on the road for a few days. Then getting hit by a car that never stopped to help him had just made his condition much worse.

"But he's a trouper. Great dog. Glad we've found the owners," Dr. Shapiro said to us before closing the door to go and get him.

George and Verna were waiting in the lobby, and my mom paced back and forth in the small room. I couldn't speak, couldn't breathe, couldn't think.

"Be Danny, Danny, Danny" was the pulsing beat in my heart. The minutes of waiting for the vet to come back felt like an eternity.

Dr. Shapiro finally opened the door with the dog by his side. "Here he is," he announced.

I looked into his eyes, then down his black and white shaggy coat to a leg that was bandaged all the way up. I watched a tail that wagged like it would never stop when he saw me. I fell on the floor and opened my arms wide as he hobbled over to me, his tail still wagging a million miles an hour. I kissed him over and over again in the fuzzy spot between his eyes.

"Danny, it's really you!" I cried into his soft fur.

"Thank the heavens above!" My mother dropped beside me and wrapped her arms around us both.

Danny barked with excitement and licked the tears from our faces over and over again, then cocked his head and gave me a look as if to say, "Hey, what took you so long?"

"You didn't exactly make it easy." I laughed. "All your adventures have to include me from now on, Danny-O." He put both paws around my neck and looked into my eyes as if to say, "Don't worry. I'm done. There's no place I'd rather be than home."

I smelled my dad's spicy aftershave as he joined us, and we remained, clinging to one another and the dog that we loved, on the white linoleum floor.

We were a family once again.

Chapter Twenty-Five

"Slow down, boy, he's still healin'." Rayleen cupped her hands around her mouth and hollered at Neptune, who was playing chase with Danny in our backyard. It had been a month since that memorable Saturday, and Dr. Shapiro had taken the bandages off just two weeks ago.

It still seemed like a dream, bringing Danny home, watching him lie down in his doggy bed for the first time. My dad went out and bought him a big delicious dog bone as a welcome-home treat, and on Monday morning my mom, Danny, and I saw my dad off at the airport. I would miss him terribly.

I relished every second of lying on the couch with Danny again, careful not to crush his leg as I watched TV and held him close.

I slept better than I had since he was gone, with my feet pressed against his furry body as he curled up, like he always did, at the bottom of my bed.

Lulu and Ashton had both been ecstatic when I text messaged them from the car that I had my dog back, with Danny resting his head in my lap as we drove home from the vet's office.

I had called Rayleen while my mom and dad said good-bye to Verna and George, and she was very quiet in a way I had never heard her before.

"That's great news, sweet pea. I'm happy for you," she said before handing the phone to Martha, who told me she was going to make Danny his own special batch of chicken and yams and rice and that he and Neptune would be best friends. They were. The dogs played together at least three times a week, and since Danny couldn't walk very far yet, I stopped by every afternoon to take Neptune to Ocean Avenue for a walk. He was a changed dog. Happy and confident and the light of Martha's life.

Kate was pretty upset that we didn't make it to her party, but Lulu and I made it up to her with the kind of day we knew she'd love. Mall shopping and a movie, then a sleepover. Yes, we were very different, but she was still one of my oldest friends.

I had gone to the shelter to volunteer with Rayleen every Saturday since our big adoption day, and New Hope Steve had even introduced me to his boss, who had decided to start a youth volunteer program at their shelter. We had another big adoption day coming up in a few weeks. Kate had even said she'd give it a try and come help out.

"I'm glad your dad's getting serious about writing his book," Rayleen said as she threw a stick to the two dogs, who gave chase after it.

It was late afternoon and the sun was at its most special color of the day, soft and golden.

"He called from Kabul and said he's writing at night," I said, looking over at Rayleen and taking in every inch of her slowly. I wanted to hold on to the memory of her, how she looked now and always: strong, sinewy arms, cargo pants, flip-flops, and wild, caramel-colored hair.

"Do you have to leave?" I felt my throat close around the words.

"Yes, sweet pea. My work here's done. New Mexico is callin'. I've placed all the rescue dogs, 'cept Clay, who I'm keeping for sentimental reasons." She cleared her throat. "I wouldn't have met you if it weren't for him." She looked out across the lawn as Neptune and Danny rolled around in the grass together.

"I wish you'd stay," I said softly.

Rayleen reached over and hugged me. "Hey, I'm leavin' the LA downtown shelter dogs in good hands. Got you and New Hope Steve runnin' the show. That's a fine team if ever I saw one."

"My mom's talked her station into letting her do an Adopt a Rescue Pet segment three mornings a week."

"That's great news, sweet pea. Told ya she was a keeper."

Danny and Neptune came bounding over and drank thirstily from the water bowl. Rayleen bent down to give Neptune and Danny a last hug good-bye.

"The note I wrote to Danny," I said. "What'd you do with it?"

She had one arm around each dog, the golden light engulfing them in a shimmering circle.

"Gave the envelope a kiss and sent it to my mama up in heaven." Rayleen looked up at me with tears in her eyes. "Knew she'd come through."

I walked Rayleen to her truck, which was loaded with her belonging and her ten dogs, including Clay. They barked and jumped up and down when they saw her and she gave a loud "Allakazam!" that made them all stop instantly.

"Magic powers," I said. "You really have them."

"We all do," she said, looking deeply into my eyes. "You just have to believe."

"Can you teach me how?"

"You're already doing it, sweet pea." She held me close as I breathed in her lavender and wet earth smell for the last time. "You already are."

Epilogue

Dear Rayleen,

Thank you for the wonderful turquoise Coyote earrings and birthday card. It's hard to believe I'm a teenager now. My mom and dad and I just got back from a week in Hawaii. I've always wanted us to go, so it was their b'day present to me. Danny stayed with Ashton and his two dogs, Buster and Bullwinkle, and they had a blast. I guess you could say Ashton is officially my boyfriend, since our dogs all get along so well. That's a joke, but hopefully he will be someday!

I'm glad the rescue work is going well in New

Mexico. Nineteen new dogs living with you plus your ten! That must be one of your all-time records. I'm sure you will find great homes for all of them.

In the months since Danny has been back I have had a lot of time to think about everything. What I've come to realize is that his disappearance was a gift in a way I could have never imagined. It took me on a journey to find him, but in my search I found you, and Martha, and New Hope Steve, and my passion for saving animals, and Ashton. It brought me closer to Lulu—we work every weekend at the shelter together—and it gave me a chance to get closer to my dad and especially, especially my mom. She only works two full days and is home with me a lot. She now does the morning "Save a Pet" segment that was totally her idea. It's a big hit with the viewers!

I would never want to lose Danny ever again, and I know we won't. He has a very secure new collar with three different phone numbers on it, and we got him microchipped. He even has a GPS system on him now. It cost a fortune, but my dad says he's more than worth it.

There's this saying that I always used to think about, and it used to make me upset. It is "The only thing in life that's constant is change." But my dad, who's in India right now, sent me this great book by

Mahatma Gandhi, and right there on the first page is a quote by him that was meant for me to see. He said, "You must be the change you wish to see in the world."

This was the lesson you taught me, Rayleen. Thank you for being my mentor and guide.

Always,
Your "sweet pea,"
Bree

Author's Note

I hope that reading my book has encouraged you to think about helping animals in need. Like Bree, becoming a volunteer with a local shelter is a great way to make a difference in an animal's life. If your family is thinking about adopting a pet, instead of going to the pet store, ask your parents to take a trip to a nearby shelter or rescue group. There are tons of shelters and rescue groups all over the country. To find one close to you simply type in "animal shelter" or "animal rescue group" along with your city and state into any search engine and you will get all the information you need.

I know it can sometimes feel overwhelming that

there are so many animals in need and that it is impossible to help them all. When I start feeling overwhelmed, I think about these words:

Saving just ONE DOG *won't change the world . . .*
but it will surely change the world of that ONE DOG.

In the words of the great political and spiritual leader of India Mahatma Gandhi, "The greatness of a nation and its moral progress can be judged by the way its animals are treated."

Many thanks,
Linzi

If you'd like to learn about my rescue dogs or get more information about rescuing animals, go to: www.theforgottendog.org

Acknowledgments

If Cary Granat had not stood in my garden, surrounded by my pack of rescue dogs, this book would never have existed. I am eternally grateful to him for his moment of inspiration and his belief in my writing and rescue life.

I am doubly blessed to have had the gentle but constructive guidance of two wonderful editors: Kellie Celia, associate editor of Walden Pond Press, whose thoughtful input was invaluable; and Jordan Brown, editor of Walden Pond Press, whose clear insights greatly helped this story. Special thanks to Walden Pond Press publisher, Chip Flaherty, and editorial director, Debbie

Kovacs, who both supported this book from its inception. A word of thanks to Amy Ryan, who designed the wonderful book jacket. My gratitude to production editor Jon Howard and copy editor Brooke Dworkin, and a nod of appreciation to Alessandra Balzer and Donna Bray, publishers of Walden Pond Press at HarperCollins.

A word of thanks to my agent, Kenneth Wright, at Writers House, who is always there when I need him.

I am fortunate to be part of an amazing group of writers that meets every Tuesday evening. Our years spent sharing pages and ideas have guided me in ways that I could never quantify. My love to Lisa Doctor, my dear friend and writing teacher, who knows me from cover to cover. A big hug to a jewel of a friend, Terri Cheney, and thanks as always to fellow S.A. writer and friend Helena Kriel, the very lovely Terry Hoffmann, and the kind and insightful Robert Rotstein for your collective creative support.

My family and friends are cherished and irreplaceable, and words cannot express my appreciation for their support. A big hug goes to my BFF, Kathy Jackoway, who remains a beautiful, permanent fixture at my side through good and bad. My love and gratitude to Barbara Mandel, whose generosity and friendship know no bounds. My thanks to good friends Patty

Wheelock and Sharon Cicero, who both have such big hearts. A huge word of thanks to my mom and dad for their unconditional support. A word of gratitude to Ron Furst, whose sane guidance keeps my feet on the ground. And a word of thanks to ex-hubby, Marvin Katz, who remains a welcome joy in my life.

Being in the trenches of animal rescue is gut wrenching, exhausting, heartbreaking, and draining—both financially and emotionally. But it is also exhilarating, extraordinary, and rewarding beyond words. There is no greater joy for those of us in rescue than uniting a shelter, street, abused, or abandoned dog with a wonderful new forever owner.

We are a group of dedicated volunteers who do this simply for the love of the animals. The rescue saints are all exceptional in their own way, but I salute those whom I have had the privilege to know and work with over the past few years. To Sylva Kelegian, my rescue mentor who showed me the way; Victoria Burrows of Starpaws Rescue, who is a huge support in every way and allows us all to have a place to show our dogs for adoptions every Sunday; Steve Spiro and Suzanna Urszuly, the gorgeous duo who never stop saving dogs; and Kris Kelly, who is fierce in her rescue convictions and generously supplies me with dog food. A huge debt of gratitude to my dog fosters Karen Dice, Barbara

Levitan, Lizza Reed, and Pam Carter. These amazing women stepped in at the eleventh hour and took in dogs that otherwise would have been euthanized or remained in awful situations. An added word of appreciation to Cappi Patterson, for all her rescue efforts; thanks to Peter James, our very special dog whisperer; to Stefanie Pelka, dedicated trainer and "Bailey" lover; to Simone Wuncher, for committing her pet store, Pet Mania, to take in and place only rescue dogs; to the beyond courageous Helen Darvall, our Sunday adoption rescue angels Suzanne Happ, Lorna and Mark Round, the Sullivan and Boland families, eleven-year-old Jackie Sanett, and Starr Barragan, who will drive anywhere to save an animal. My gratitude to Tomika Johnson, New Hope Coordinator at the South Los Angeles shelter, who fights every day to save the lives of red listed animals, and fabulous dog sitter Chrissy Giardini, who stops in and takes over whenever I travel. Special thanks to officer Dancie Shepherd at the Santa Monica shelter, who is a true animal lover. A big thanks to Dr. Gary Adams of Westside Emergency Animal Hospital for truly giving the best medical care to sick rescue dogs and reducing costs drastically. There are many, many more, but my special thanks to these selfless men and women.

My love and appreciation to my daughter, Jordan, who has put up with many a pair of chewed shoes, stepping into "accidents," and accompanying me on rescue missions when she is home from college in New York.

And lastly, a loving thanks to my high-strung, four-pound Chihuahua, Preston, who was saved from the mean streets of Compton more than six years ago and became my very first rescue dog. If it were not for you, my sweet boy, I would not have saved all the dogs that I have since the day you were placed in my arms.

Get Active for Animals!

Young people across the country
speak up for animals in need.
You can too—join **Mission: Humane**!

Join **Mission: Humane** to take part in projects to protect animals, learn how to form a club, and get fun rewards for taking action! Projects include:

A Cause for Paws. Learn about dog care and help stop cruel puppy mills.
Combat Cruelty. Raise awareness about the need for stronger laws.
Friends for Hens. Educate others about the cruelty of battery cages. Birds kept in these small cages can't walk or even spread their wings!
Shoot to Save Wildlife. Take photos of your wild animal neighbors, and use them to teach others to live peacefully with wildlife.
Coats for Cubs. Raise awareness about the cruelty of fur in clothing.

***KIND* News**. To learn more about animal issues and what kids are doing to help, read KIND News! It features fascinating articles, puzzles, projects, and interviews with celebrities who are also actively working to help animals.

To learn how to join Mission: Humane visit
www.humanesociety.org/kids.
The animals are waiting for your help!